A Ride Across Palestine

&

An Unprotected Female at the Pyramids

ANTHONY TROLLOPE

Serenity
Publishers, LLC
ROCKVILLE, MARYLAND
2009

ISBN: 978-1-60450-654-9

Published by Serenity Publishers
An Arc Manor Company
P. O. Box 10339
Rockville, MD 20849-0339
www.SerenityPublishers.com

Printed in the United States of America/United Kingdom

CONTENTS

A RIDE ACROSS PALESTINE   5

AN UNPROTECTED FEMALE AT THE PYRAMIDS   55

A RIDE ACROSS PALESTINE

Circumstances took me to the Holy Land without a companion, and compelled me to visit Bethany, the Mount of Olives, and the Church of the Sepulchre alone. I acknowledge myself to be a gregarious animal, or, perhaps, rather one of those which nature has intended to go in pairs. At any rate I dislike solitude, and especially travelling solitude, and was, therefore, rather sad at heart as I sat one night at Z-'s hotel, in Jerusalem, thinking over my proposed wanderings for the next few days. Early on the following morning I intended to start, of course on horseback, for the Dead Sea, the banks of Jordan, Jericho, and those mountains of the wilderness through which it is supposed that Our Saviour wandered for the forty days when the devil tempted him. I would then return to the Holy City, and remaining only long enough to refresh my horse and wipe the dust from my hands and feet, I would start again for Jaffa, and there catch a certain Austrian steamer which would take me to Egypt. Such was my programme, and I confess that I was but ill contented with it, seeing that I was to be alone during the time.

I had already made all my arrangements, and though I had no reason for any doubt as to my personal security during the trip, I did not feel altogether satisfied with them. I intended to take a French guide, or dragoman, who had been with me for some days, and to put myself under the peculiar guardianship of two Bedouin Arabs, who were to accompany me as long as I should remain east of Jerusalem. This travelling through the desert under the protection of Bedouins was, in idea, pleasant enough; and I must here declare that I did not at all begrudge the forty shillings which I was told by our British consul that I must pay them for their trouble, in accordance with the established tariff. But I did begrudge the fact of the tariff. I would rather have fallen in with my friendly Arabs, as it were by chance, and have rewarded their fidelity at the end of our joint journeyings by a donation of piastres to be settled by myself, and which, under such circumstances, would certainly have been as agreeable to them as the stipulated sum. In the same way I dislike having waiters put down in my bill. I find that I pay them twice over, and thus lose money; and as they do not expect to be so treated, I never have the advantage of their civility. The world, I fear, is becoming too fond of tariffs.

"A tariff!" said I to the consul, feeling that the whole romance of my expedition would be dissipated by such an arrangement. "Then I'll go alone; I'll take a revolver with me."

"You can't do it, sir," said the consul, in a dry and somewhat angry tone. "You have no more right to ride through that country without paying the regular price for protection, than you have to stop in Z—'s hotel without settling the bill."

I could not contest the point, so I ordered my Bedouins for the appointed day, exactly as I would send for a ticket-porter at home, and determined to make the best of it. The wild unlimited sands, the desolation of the Dead Sea, the rushing waters of Jordan, the outlines of the mountains of Moab;—those things the consular tariff could not alter, nor deprive them of the glories of their association.

I had submitted, and the arrangements had been made. Joseph, my dragoman, was to come to me with the horses and an Arab groom at five in the morning, and we were to encounter our Bedouins outside the gate of St. Stephen, down the hill, where the road turns, close to the tomb of the Virgin.

I was sitting alone in the public room at the hotel, filling my flask with brandy,—for matters of primary importance I never leave to servant, dragoman, or guide,—when the waiter entered, and said that a gentleman wished to speak with me. The gentleman had not sent in his card or name; but any gentleman was welcome to me in my solitude, and I requested that the gentleman might enter. In appearance the gentleman certainly was a gentleman, for I thought that I had never before seen a young man whose looks were more in his favour, or whose face and gait and outward bearing seemed to betoken better breeding. He might be some twenty or twenty-one years of age, was slight and well made, with very black hair, which he wore rather long, very dark long bright eyes, a straight nose, and teeth that were perfectly white. He was dressed throughout in grey tweed clothing, having coat, waistcoat, and trousers of the same; and in his hand he carried a very broad-brimmed straw hat.

"Mr. Jones, I believe," he said, as he bowed to me. Jones is a good travelling name, and, if the reader will allow me, I will call myself Jones on the present occasion.

"Yes," I said, pausing with the brandy-bottle in one hand, and the flask in the other. "That's my name; I'm Jones. Can I do anything for you, sir?"

"Why, yes, you can," said he. "My name is Smith,— John Smith."

"Pray sit down, Mr. Smith," I said, pointing to a chair. "Will you do anything in this way?" and I proposed to hand the bottle to him. "As far as I can judge from a short stay, you won't find much like that in Jerusalem."

He declined the Cognac, however, and immediately began his story. "I hear, Mr. Jones," said he, "that you are going to Moab to-morrow."

"Well," I replied, "I don't know whether I shall cross the water. It's not very easy, I take it, at all times; but I shall certainly get as far as Jordan. Can I do anything for you in those parts?"

And then he explained to me what was the object of his visit. He was quite alone in Jerusalem, as I was myself; and was staying at H—'s hotel. He had heard that I was starting for the Dead Sea, and had called to ask if I objected to his joining me. He had found himself, he said, very lonely; and as he had heard that I also was alone, he had ventured to call and make his proposition. He seemed to be very bashful, and half ashamed of what he was doing; and when he had done speaking he declared himself conscious that he was intruding, and expressed a hope that I would not hesitate to say so if his suggestion were from any cause disagreeable to me.

As a rule I am rather shy of chance travelling English friends. It has so frequently happened to me that I have had to blush for the acquaintances whom I have selected, that I seldom indulge in any close intimacies of this kind. But, nevertheless, I was taken with John Smith, in spite of his name. There was so much about him that was pleasant, both to the eye and to the understanding! One meets constantly with men from contact with whom one revolts without knowing the cause of such dislike. The cut of their beard is displeasing, or the mode in which they walk or speak. But, on the other hand, there are men who are attractive, and I must confess that I was attracted by John Smith at first sight. I hesitated, however, for a minute; for there are sundry things of which it behoves a traveller to think before he can join a companion for such a journey as that which I was about to make. Could the young man rise early, and remain in the saddle for ten hours together? Could he live upon hard-boiled eggs and brandy-and-water? Could he take his chance of a tent under which to sleep, and make himself happy with the bare fact of being in the desert? He saw my hesitation, and attributed it to a cause which was not present in my mind at the moment, though the subject was one of the greatest importance when strangers consent to join themselves together for a time, and agree to become no strangers on the spur of the moment.

"Of course I will take half the expense," said he, absolutely blushing as he mentioned the matter.

"As to that there will be very little. You have your own horse, of course?"

"Oh, yes."

"My dragoman and groom-boy will do for both. But you'll have to pay forty shillings to the Arabs! There's no getting over that. The consul won't even look after your dead body, if you get murdered, without going through that ceremony."

Mr. Smith immediately produced his purse, which he tendered to me. "If you will manage it all," said he, "it will make it so much the easier, and I shall be infinitely obliged to you." This of course I declined to do. I had no business with his purse, and explained to him that if we went together we could settle that on our return to Jerusalem. "But could he go through really hard work?" I asked. He answered me with an assurance that he would and could do anything in that way that it was possible for man to perform. As for eating and drinking he cared nothing about it, and would undertake to be astir at any hour of the morning that might be named. As for sleeping accommodation, he did not care if he kept his clothes on for a week together. He looked slight and weak; but he spoke so well, and that without boasting, that I ultimately agreed to his proposal, and in a few minutes he took his leave of me, promising to be at Z-'s door with his horse at five o'clock on the following morning.

"I wish you'd allow me to leave my purse with you," he said again.

"I cannot think of it. There is no possible occasion for it," I said again. "If there is anything to pay, I'll ask you for it when the journey is over. That forty shillings you must fork out. It's a law of the Medes and Persians."

"I'd better give it you at once," he said again, offering me money. But I would not have it. It would be quite time enough for that when the Arabs were leaving us.

"Because," he added, "strangers, I know, are sometimes suspicious about money; and I would not, for worlds, have you think that I would put you to expense." I assured him that I did not think so, and then the subject was dropped.

He was, at any rate, up to his time, for when I came down on the following morning I found him in the narrow street, the first on horseback. Joseph, the Frenchman, was strapping on to a rough pony our belongings, and was staring at Mr. Smith. My new friend, unfortunately, could not speak a word of French, and therefore I had to explain to the dragoman how it had come to pass that our party was to be enlarged.

"But the Bedouins will expect full pay for both," said he, alarmed. Men in that class, and especially Orientals, always think that every arrangement of life, let it be made in what way it will, is made with the intention of saving some expense, or cheating somebody out of some money. They do not understand that men can have any other object, and are ever on their guard lest the saving should be made at their cost, or lest they should be the victims of the fraud.

"All right," said I.

"I shall be responsible, Monsieur," said the dragoman, piteously.

"It shall be all right," said I, again. "If that does not satisfy you, you may remain behind."

"If Monsieur says it is all right, of course it is so;" and then he completed his strapping. We took blankets with us, of which I had to borrow two out of the hotel for my friend Smith, a small hamper of provisions, a sack containing forage for the horses, and a large empty jar, so that we might supply ourselves with water when leaving the neighbourhood of wells for any considerable time.

"I ought to have brought these things for myself," said Smith, quite unhappy at finding that he had thrown on me the necessity of catering for him. But I laughed at him, saying that it was nothing; he should do as much for me another time. I am prepared to own that I do not willingly rush up-stairs and load myself with blankets out of strange rooms for men whom I do not know; nor, as a rule, do I make all the Smiths of the world free of my canteen. But, with reference to this fellow I did feel more than ordinarily good-natured and unselfish. There was something in the tone of his voice which was satisfactory; and I should really have felt vexed had anything occurred at the last moment to prevent his going with me.

Let it be a rule with every man to carry an English saddle with him when travelling in the East. Of what material is formed the nether man of a Turk I have never been informed, but I am sure that it is not flesh and blood. No flesh and blood,—simply flesh and blood,—could withstand the wear and tear of a Turkish saddle. This being the case, and the consequences being well known to me, I was grieved to find that Smith was not properly provided. He was seated on one of those hard, red, high-pointed machines, in which the shovels intended to act as stirrups are attached in such a manner, and hang at such an angle, as to be absolutely destructive to the leg of a Christian. There is no part of the Christian body with which the Turkish saddle comes in contact that does not become more or less macerated. I have sat in one for days, but I left it a flayed man; and, therefore, I was sorry for Smith.

I explained this to him, taking hold of his leg by the calf to show how the leather would chafe him; but it seemed to me that he did not quite like my interference. "Never mind," said he, twitching his leg away, "I have ridden in this way before."

"Then you must have suffered the very mischief?"

"Only a little, and I shall be used to it now. You will not hear me complain."

"By heavens, you might have heard me complain a mile off when I came to the end of a journey I once took. I roared like a bull when I began to cool. Joseph, could you not get a European saddle for Mr. Smith?" But Joseph did not seem to like Mr. Smith, and declared such a thing to be impossible. No European in Jerusalem would think of lending so precious an article, except to a very dear friend. Joseph himself was on an English saddle, and I made up my mind that after the first stage, we would bribe him to make an exchange. And then we started.

The Bedouins were not with us, but we were to meet them, as I have said before, outside St. Stephen's gate. "And if they are not there," said Joseph, "we shall be sure to come across them on the road."

"Not there!" said I. "How about the consul's tariff, if they don't keep their part of the engagement?" But Joseph explained to me that their part of the engagement really amounted to this,—that we should ride into their country without molestation, provided that such and such payments were made.

It was the period of Easter, and Jerusalem was full of pilgrims. Even at that early hour of the morning we could hardly make our way through the narrow streets. It must be understood that there is no accommodation in the town for the fourteen or fifteen thousand strangers who flock to the Holy Sepulchre at this period of the year. Many of them sleep out in the open air, lying on low benches which run along the outside walls of the houses, or even on the ground, wrapped in their thick hoods and cloaks. Slumberers such as these are easily disturbed, nor are they detained long at their toilets. They shake themselves like dogs, and growl and stretch themselves, and then they are ready for the day.

We rode out of the town in a long file. First went the groom-boy; I forget his proper Syrian appellation, but we used to call him Mucherry, that sound being in some sort like the name. Then followed the horse with the forage and blankets, and next to him my friend Smith in the Turkish saddle. I was behind him, and Joseph brought up the rear. We moved slowly down the Via Dolorosa, noting the spot at which our Saviour is said to have fallen while bearing his cross; we passed by Pilate's house, and paused at the gate of the Temple,—the gate which once was beautiful,—looking down into the hole of the pool in which the maimed and halt were healed whenever the waters moved. What names they are! And yet there at Jerusalem they are bandied to and fro with as little reverence as are the fanciful appellations given by guides to rocks and stones and little lakes in all countries overrun by tourists.

"For those who would still fain believe,—let them stay at home," said my friend Smith.

"For those who cannot divide the wheat from the chaff, let *them* stay at home," I answered. And then we rode out through St. Stephen's gate, having the mountain of the men of Galilee directly before us, and the Mount of Olives a little to our right, and the Valley of Jehoshaphat lying between us and it. "Of course you know all these places now?" said Smith. I answered that I did know them well.

"And was it not better for you when you knew them only in Holy Writ?" he asked.

"No, by Jove," said I. "The mountains stand where they ever stood. The same valleys are still green with the morning dew, and the water-courses are unchanged. The children of Mahomet may build their tawdry temple on the threshing-floor which David bought that there might stand the Lord's house. Man may undo what man did, even though the doer was Solomon. But here we have God's handiwork and His own evidences."

At the bottom of the steep descent from the city gate we came to the tomb of the Virgin; and by special agreement made with Joseph we left our horses here for a few moments, in order that we might descend into the subterranean chapel under the tomb, in which mass was at this moment being said. There is something awful in that chapel, when, as at the present moment, it is crowded with Eastern worshippers from the very altar up to the top of the dark steps by which the descent is made. It must be remembered that Eastern worshippers are not like the churchgoers of London, or even of Rome or Cologne. They are wild men of various nations and races,—Maronites from Lebanon Roumelians, Candiotes, Copts from Upper Egypt, Russians from the Crimea, Armenians and Abyssinians. They savour strongly of Oriental life and of Oriental dirt. They are clad in skins or hairy cloaks with huge hoods. Their heads are shaved, and their faces covered with short, grisly, fierce beards. They are silent mostly, looking out of their eyes ferociously, as though murder were in their thoughts, and rapine. But they never slouch, or cringe in their bodies, or shuffle in their gait. Dirty, fierce-looking, uncouth, repellent as they are, there is always about them a something of personal dignity which is not compatible with an Englishman's ordinary hat and pantaloons.

As we were about to descend, preparing to make our way through the crowd, Smith took hold of my arm. "That will never do, my dear fellow," said I, "the job will be tough enough for a single file, but we should never cut our way two and two. I'm broad-shouldered and will go first." So I did, and gradually we worked our way into the body of the chapel. How is it that Englishmen can push themselves anywhere? These men were fierce-looking, and had murder and rapine, as I have said, almost in their eyes. One would have supposed that they were not lambs or doves, capable of being thrust here or there without anger on their part; and they, too, were all anxious to descend and approach the altar. Yet we did win our way through them, and apparently no man was angry with us. I doubt, after all, whether a ferocious eye and a strong smell and dirt are so efficacious in creating awe and obedience in others, as an open brow and traces of soap and water. I know this, at least,—that a dirty Maronite would make very little progress, if he attempted to shove his way unfairly through a crowd of Englishmen at the door of a London theatre. We did shove unfairly, and we did make progress, till we found ourselves in the centre of the dense crowd collected in the body of the chapel.

Having got so far, our next object was to get out again. The place was dark, mysterious, and full of strange odours; but darkness, mystery, and strange odours soon lose their charms when men have much work before them. Joseph had made a point of being allowed to attend mass before the altar of the Virgin, but a very few minutes sufficed for his prayers. So we again turned round and pushed our way back again, Smith still following in my wake. The men who had let us pass once let us pass again without opposition or show of anger. To them the occasion was very holy. They were stretching out their hands in every direction, with long tapers, in order that they might obtain a spark of the sacred fire which was burning on one of the altars. As we made our way out we passed many who, with dumb motions, begged us to assist them in their object. And we did assist them, getting lights for their tapers, handing them to and fro, and using the authority with which we seemed to be invested. But Smith, I observed, was much more courteous in this way to the women than to the men, as I did not forget to remind him when we were afterwards on our road together.

Remounting our horses we rode slowly up the winding ascent of the Mount of Olives, turning round at the brow of the hill to look back over Jerusalem. Sometimes I think that of all spots in the world this one should be the spot most cherished in the memory of Christians. It was there that He stood when He wept over the city. So much we do know, though we are ignorant, and ever shall be so, of the site of His cross and of the tomb. And then we descended on the eastern side of the hill, passing through Bethany, the town of Lazarus and his sisters, and turned our faces steadily towards the mountains of Moab.

Hitherto we had met no Bedouins, and I interrogated my dragoman about them more than once; but he always told me that it did not signify; we should meet them, he said, before any danger could arise. "As for danger," said I, "I think more of this than I do of the Arabs," and I put my hand on my revolver. "But as they agreed to be here, here they ought to be. Don't you carry a revolver, Smith?"

Smith said that he never had done so, but that he would take the charge of mine if I liked. To this, however, I demurred. "I never part with my pistol to any one," I said, rather drily. But he explained that he only intended to signify that if there were danger to be encountered, he would be glad to encounter it; and I fully believed him. "We shan't have much fighting," I replied; "but if there be any, the tool will come readiest to the hand of its master. But if you mean to remain here long I would advise you to get one. These Orientals are a people with whom appearances go a long way, and, as a rule, fear and respect mean the same thing with them. A pistol hanging over your loins is no great trouble to you, and looks as though you could bite. Many a dog goes through the world well by merely showing his teeth."

And then my companion began to talk of himself. "He did not," he said, "mean to remain in Syria very long."

"Nor I either," said I. "I have done with this part of the world for the present, and shall take the next steamer from Jaffa for Alexandria. I shall only have one night in Jerusalem on my return."

After this he remained silent for a few moments and then declared that that also had been his intention. He was almost ashamed to say so, however, because it looked as though he had resolved to hook himself on to me. So he answered, expressing almost regret at the circumstance.

"Don't let that trouble you," said I; "I shall be delighted to have your company. When you know me better, as I hope you will do, you will find that if such were not the case I should tell you so as frankly. I shall remain in Cairo some little time; so that beyond our arrival in Egypt, I can answer for nothing."

He said that he expected letters at Alexandria which would govern his future movements. I thought he seemed sad as he said so, and imagined, from his manner, that he did not expect very happy tidings. Indeed

I had made up my mind that he was by no means free from care or sorrow. He had not the air of a man who could say of himself that he was "totus teres atque rotundus." But I had no wish to inquire, and the matter would have dropped had he not himself added—"I fear that I shall meet acquaintances in Egypt whom it will give me no pleasure to see."

"Then," said I, "if I were you, I would go to Constantinople instead;—indeed, anywhere rather than fall among friends who are not friendly. And the nearer the friend is, the more one feels that sort of thing. To my way of thinking, there is nothing on earth so pleasant as a pleasant wife; but then, what is there so damnable as one that is unpleasant?"

"Are you a married man?" he inquired. All his questions were put in a low tone of voice which seemed to give to them an air of special interest, and made one almost feel that they were asked with some special view to one's individual welfare. Now the fact is, that I am a married man with a family; but I am not much given to talk to strangers about my domestic concerns, and, therefore, though I had no particular object in view, I denied my obligations in this respect. "No," said I; "I have not come to that promotion yet. I am too frequently on the move to write myself down as Paterfamilias."

"Then you know nothing about that pleasantness of which you spoke just now?"

"Nor of the unpleasantness, thank God; my personal experiences are all to come,—as also are yours, I presume?"

It was possible that he had hampered himself with some woman, and that she was to meet him at Alexandria. Poor fellow! thought I. But his unhappiness was not of that kind. "No," said he; "I am not married; I am all alone in the world."

"Then I certainly would not allow myself to be troubled by unpleasant acquaintances."

It was now four hours since we had left Jerusalem, and we had arrived at the place at which it was proposed that we should breakfast. There was a large well there, and shade afforded by a rock under which the water sprung; and the Arabs had constructed a tank out of which the horses could drink, so that the place was ordinarily known as the first stage out of Jerusalem.

Smith had said not a word about his saddle, or complained in any way of discomfort, so that I had in truth forgotten the subject. Other matters had continually presented themselves, and I had never even asked him how he had fared. I now jumped from my horse, but I perceived at once that he was unable to do so. He smiled faintly, as his eye caught mine, but I knew that he wanted assistance. "Ah," said I, "that confounded Turkish saddle has already galled your skin. I see how it is; I shall have to doctor you with a little brandy,—externally applied, my friend." But I lent him my shoulder, and with that assistance he got down, very gently and slowly.

We ate our breakfast with a good will; bread and cold fowl and brandy-and-water, with a hard-boiled egg by way of a final delicacy; and then I began to bargain with Joseph for the loan of his English saddle. I saw that Smith could not get through the journey with that monstrous Turkish affair, and that he would go on without complaining till he fainted or came to some other signal grief. But the Frenchman, seeing the plight in which we were, was disposed to drive a very hard bargain. He wanted forty shillings, the price of a pair of live Bedouins, for the accommodation, and declared that, even then, he should make the sacrifice only out of consideration to me.

"Very well," said I. "I'm tolerably tough myself; and I'll change with the gentleman. The chances are that I shall not be in a very liberal humour when I reach Jaffa with stiff limbs and a sore skin. I have a very good memory, Joseph."

"I'll take thirty shillings, Mr. Jones; though I shall have to groan all the way like a condemned devil."

I struck a bargain with him at last for five-and-twenty, and set him to work to make the necessary change on the horses. "It will be just the same thing to him," I said to Smith. "I find that he is as much used to one as to the other."

"But how much money are you to pay him?" he asked. "Oh, nothing," I replied. "Give him a few piastres when you part with him at Jaffa." I do not know why I should have felt thus inclined to pay money out of my pocket for this Smith,—a man whom I had only seen for the first time on the preceding evening, and whose temperament was so essentially different from my own; but so I did. I would have done almost anything in reason for his comfort; and yet he was a melancholy fellow, with good inward pluck as I believed, but without that outward show of dash and hardihood which I confess I love to see. "Pray tell him that I'll pay him for it," said he. "We'll make that all right," I answered; and then we remounted,—not without some difficulty on his part. "You should have let me rub in that brandy," I said. "You can't conceive how efficaciously I would have done it." But he made me no answer.

At noon we met a caravan of pilgrims coming up from Jordan. There might be some three or four hundred, but the number seemed to be treble that, from the loose and straggling line in which they journeyed. It was a very singular sight, as they moved slowly along the narrow path through the sand, coming out of a defile among the hills, which was perhaps a quarter of a mile in front of us, passing us as we stood still by the wayside, and then winding again out of sight on the track over which we had come. Some rode on camels,—a whole family, in many cases, being perched on the same animal. I observed a very old man and a very old woman slung in panniers over a camel's back,—not such panniers as might be befitting such a purpose, but square baskets, so that the heads and heels of each of the old couple hung out of the rear and front. "Surely the journey will be their death," I said to Joseph. "Yes it will," he replied, quite coolly; "but what matter how soon they die now that they have bathed in Jordan?" Very many rode on donkeys; two, generally, on each donkey; others, who had command of money, on horses; but the greater number walked, toiling painfully from Jerusalem to Jericho on the first day, sleeping there in tents and going to bathe on the second day, and then returning from Jericho to Jerusalem on the third. The pilgrimage is made throughout in accordance with fixed rules, and there is a tariff for the tent accommodation at Jericho,—so much per head per night, including the use of hot water.

Standing there, close by the wayside, we could see not only the garments and faces of these strange people, but we could watch their gestures and form some opinion of what was going on within their thoughts. They were much quieter,—tamer, as it were,—than Englishmen would be under such circumstances. Those who were carried seemed to sit on their beasts in passive tranquillity, neither enjoying nor suffering anything. Their object had been to wash in Jordan,—to do that once in their lives;—and they had washed in Jordan. The benefit expected was not to be immediately spiritual. No earnest prayerfulness was considered necessary after the ceremony. To these members of the Greek Christian Church it had been handed down from father to son that washing in Jordan once during life was efficacious towards salvation. And therefore the journey had been made at terrible cost and terrible risk; for these people had come from afar, and were from their habits but little capable of long journeys. Many die under the toil; but this matters not if they do not die before they have reached Jordan. Some few there are, undoubtedly, more ecstatic in this great deed of their religion. One man I especially noticed on this day. He had bound himself to make the pilgrimage from Jerusalem to the river with one foot bare. He was of a better class, and was even nobly dressed, as though it were a part of his vow to show to all men that he did this deed, wealthy and great though he was. He was a fine man, perhaps thirty years of age, with a well-grown beard descending on his breast, and at his girdle he carried a brace of pistols.

But never in my life had I seen bodily pain so plainly written in a man's face. The sweat was falling from his brow, and his eyes were strained and bloodshot with agony. He had no stick, his vow, I presume, debarring him from such assistance, and he limped along, putting to the ground the heel of the unprotected foot. I could see it, and it was a mass of blood, and sores, and broken skin. An Irish girl would walk from Jerusalem to Jericho without shoes, and be not a penny the worse for it. This poor fellow clearly suffered so much that I was almost inclined to think that in the performance of his penance he had done something to aggravate his pain. Those around him paid no attention to him, and the dragoman seemed to think nothing of the affair whatever. "Those fools of Greeks do not understand the Christian religion," he said, being himself a Latin or Roman Catholic.

At the tail of the line we encountered two Bedouins, who were in charge of the caravan, and Joseph at once addressed them. The men were mounted, one on a very sorry-looking jade, but the other on a good stout Arab barb. They had guns slung behind their backs, coloured handkerchiefs on their heads, and they wore the striped bernouse. The parley went on for about ten minutes, during which the procession of pilgrims wound out of sight; and it ended in our being accompanied by the two Arabs, who thus left their greater charge to take care of itself back to the city. I understood afterwards that they had endeavoured to persuade Joseph that we might just as well go on alone, merely satisfying the demand of the tariff. But he had pointed out that I was a particular man, and that under such circumstances the final settlement might be doubtful. So they turned and accompanied us; but, as a matter of fact, we should have been as well without them.

The sun was beginning to fall in the heavens when we reached the actual margin of the Dead Sea. We had seen the glitter of its still waters for a long time previously, shining under the sun as though it were not real. We have often heard, and some of us have seen, how effects of light and shade together will produce so vivid an appearance of water where there is no water, as to deceive the most experienced. But the reverse was the case here. There was the lake, and there it had been before our eyes for the last two hours; and yet it looked, then and now, as though it were an image of a lake, and not real water. I had long since made up my mind to bathe in it, feeling well convinced that I could do so without harm to myself, and I had been endeavouring to persuade Smith to accompany me; but he positively refused. He would bathe, he said, neither in the Dead Sea nor in the river Jordan. He did not like bathing, and preferred to do his washing in his own room. Of course I had nothing further to say, and begged that, under these circumstances, he would take charge of my purse and pistols while I was in the water. This he agreed to do; but even in this he was strange and almost uncivil. I was to bathe from the farthest point of a little island, into which there was a rough cause-way from the land made of stones and broken pieces of wood, and I exhorted him to go with me thither; but he insisted on remaining with his horse on the mainland at some little distance from the island. He did not feel inclined to go down to the water's edge, he said.

I confess that at this moment I almost suspected that he was going to play me foul, and I hesitated. He saw in an instant what was passing through my mind. "You had better take your pistol and money with you; they will be quite safe on your clothes." But to have kept the things now would have shown suspicion too plainly, and as I could not bring myself to do that, I gave them up. I have sometimes thought that I was a fool to do so.

I went away by myself to the end of the island, and then I did bathe. It is impossible to conceive anything more desolate than the appearance of the place. The land shelves very gradually away to the water, and the whole margin, to the breadth of some twenty or thirty feet, is strewn with the debris of rushes, bits of timber, and old white withered reeds. Whence these bits of timber have come it seems difficult to say. The appearance is as though the water had receded and left them there. I have heard it said that there is no vegetation near the Dead Sea; but such is not the case, for these rushes do grow on the bank. I found it difficult enough to get into the water, for the ground shelves down very slowly, and is rough with stones and large pieces of half-rotten wood; moreover, when I was in nearly up to my hips the water knocked me down; indeed, it did so when I had gone as far as my knees, but I recovered myself; and by perseverance did proceed somewhat farther. It must not be imagined that this knocking down was effected by the movement of the water. There is no such movement. Everything is perfectly still, and the fluid seems hardly to be displaced by the entrance of the body; but the effect is that one's feet are tripped up, and that one falls prostrate on to the surface. The water is so strong and buoyant, that, when above a few feet in depth has to be encountered, the strength and weight of the bather are not sufficient to keep down his feet and legs. I then essayed to swim; but I could not do this in the ordinary way, as I was unable to keep enough of my body below the surface; so that my head and face seemed to be propelled down upon it.

I turned round and floated, but the glare of the sun was so powerful that I could not remain long in that position. However, I had bathed in the Dead Sea, and was so far satisfied.

Anything more abominable to the palate than this water, if it be water, I never had inside my mouth. I expected it to be extremely salt, and no doubt, if it were analysed, such would be the result; but there is a flavour in it which kills the salt. No attempt can be made at describing this taste. It may be imagined that I did not drink heartily, merely taking up a drop or two with my tongue from the palm of my hand; but it seemed to me as though I had been drenched with it. Even brandy would not relieve me from it. And then my whole body was in a mess, and I felt as though I had been rubbed with pitch. Looking at my limbs, I saw no sign on them of the fluid. They seemed to dry from this as they usually do from any other water; but still the feeling remained. However, I was to ride from hence to a spot on the banks of Jordan, which I should reach in an hour, and at which I would wash; so I clothed myself, and prepared for my departure.

Seated in my position in the island I was unable to see what was going on among the remainder of the party, and therefore could not tell whether my pistols and money was safe. I dressed, therefore, rather hurriedly, and on getting again to the shore, found that Mr. John Smith had not levanted. He was seated on his horse at some distance from Joseph and the Arabs, and had no appearance of being in league with those, no doubt, worthy guides. I certainly had suspected a ruse, and now was angry with myself that I had done so; and yet, in London, one would not trust one's money to a stranger whom one had met twenty-four hours since in a coffee-room! Why, then, do it with a stranger whom one chanced to meet in a desert?

"Thanks," I said, as he handed me my belongings. "I wish I could have induced you to come in also. The Dead Sea is now at your elbow, and, therefore, you think nothing of it; but in ten or fifteen years' time, you would be glad to be able to tell your children that you had bathed in it."

"I shall never have any children to care for such tidings," he replied.

The river Jordan, for some miles above the point at which it joins the Dead Sea, runs through very steep banks,—banks which are almost precipitous,—and is, as it were, guarded by the thick trees and bushes which grow upon its sides. This is so much the case, that one may ride, as we did, for a considerable distance along the margin, and not be able even to approach the water. I had a fancy for bathing in some spot of my own selection, instead of going to the open shore frequented by all the pilgrims; but I was baffled in this. When I did force my way down to the river side, I found that the water ran so rapidly, and that the bushes and boughs of trees grew so far over and into the stream, as to make it impossible for me to bathe. I could not have got in without my clothes, and having got in, I could not have got out again. I was, therefore obliged to put up with the open muddy shore to which the bathers descend, and at which we may presume that Joshua passed when he came over as one of the twelve spies to spy out the land. And even here I could not go full into the stream as I would fain have done, lest I should be carried down, and so have assisted to whiten the shores of the Dead Sea with my bones. As to getting over to the Moabitish side of the river, that was plainly impossible; and, indeed, it seemed to be the prevailing opinion that the passage of the river was not practicable without going up as far as Samaria. And yet we know that there, or thereabouts, the Israelites did cross it.

I jumped from my horse the moment I got to the place, and once more gave my purse and pistols to my friend. "You are going to bathe again?" he said. "Certainly," said I; "you don't suppose that I would come to Jordan and not wash there, even if I were not foul with the foulness of the Dead Sea!" "You'll kill yourself, in your present state of heat;" he said, remonstrating just as one's mother or wife might do. But even had it been my mother or wife I could not have attended to such remonstrance then; and before he had done looking at me with those big eyes of his, my coat and waistcoat and cravat were on the ground, and I was at work at my braces; whereupon he turned from me slowly, and strolled away into the wood. On this occasion I had no base fears about my money.

And then I did bathe,—very uncomfortably. The shore was muddy with the feet of the pilgrims, and the river so rapid that I hardly dared to get beyond the mud. I did manage to take a plunge in, head—foremost, but I was forced to wade out through the dirt and slush, so that I found it difficult to make my feet and legs clean enough for my shoes and stockings; and then, moreover, the flies plagued me most unmercifully. I should have thought that the filthy flavour from the Dead Sea would have saved me from that nuisance; but the mosquitoes thereabouts are probably used to it. Finding this process of bathing to be so difficult, I inquired as to the practice of the pilgrims. I found that with them, bathing in Jordan has come to be much the same as baptism has with us. It does not mean immersion. No doubt they do take off their shoes and stockings; but they do not strip, and go bodily into the water.

As soon as I was dressed I found that Smith was again at my side with purse and pistols. We then went up a little above the wood, and sat down together on the long sandy grass. It was now quite evening, so that the short Syrian twilight had commenced, and the sun was no longer hot in the heavens. It would be night as we rode on to the tents at Jericho; but there was no difficulty as to the way, and therefore we did not hurry the horses, who were feeding on the grass. We sat down together on a spot from which we could see the stream,—close together, so that when I stretched myself out in my weariness, as I did before we started, my head rested on his legs. Ah, me! one does not take such liberties with new friends in England. It was a place which led one on to some special thoughts. The mountains of Moab were before us, very plain in their outline.

"Moab is my wash-pot, and over Edom will I cast out my shoe!" There they were before us, very visible to the eye, and we began naturally to ask questions of each other. Why was Moab the wash-pot, and Edom thus cursed with indignity? Why had the right bank of the river been selected for such great purposes, whereas the left was thus condemned? Was there, at that time, any special fertility in this land of promise which has since departed from it? We are told of a bunch of grapes which took two men to carry it; but now there is not a vine in the whole country side. Now-a-days the sandy plain round Jericho is as dry and arid as are any of the valleys of Moab. The Jordan was running beneath our feet,—the Jordan in which the leprous king had washed, though the bright rivers of his own Damascus were so much nearer to his hand. It was but a humble stream to which he was sent; but the spot probably was higher up, above the Sea of Galilee, where the river is narrow. But another also had come down to this river, perhaps to this very spot on its shores, and submitted Himself to its waters;—as to whom, perhaps, it will be better that I should not speak much in this light story.

The Dead Sea was on our right, still glittering in the distance, and behind us lay the plains of Jericho and the wretched collection of huts which still bears the name of the ancient city. Beyond that, but still seemingly within easy distance of us, were the mountains of the wilderness. The wilderness! In truth, the spot was one which did lead to many thoughts.

We talked of these things, as to many of which I found that my friend was much more free in his doubts and questionings than myself; and then our words came back to ourselves, the natural centre of all men's-thoughts and words. "From what you say," I said, "I gather that you have had enough of this land?"

"Quite enough," he said. "Why seek such spots as these, if they only dispel the associations and veneration of one's childhood?"

"But with me such associations and veneration are riveted the stronger by seeing the places, and putting my hand upon the spots. I do not speak of that fictitious marble slab up there; but here, among the sandhills by this river, and at the Mount of Olives over which we passed, I do believe."

He paused a moment, and then replied: "To me it is all nothing,—absolutely nothing. But then do we not know that our thoughts are formed, and our beliefs modelled, not on the outward signs or intrinsic evidences of things,—as would be the case were we always rational,—but by the inner workings of the mind itself? At the present turn of my life I can believe in nothing that is gracious."

"Ah, you mean that you are unhappy. You have come to grief in some of your doings or belongings, and therefore find that all things are bitter to the taste. I have had my palate out of order too; but the proper appreciation of flavours has come back to me. Bah,—how noisome was that Dead Sea water!"

"The Dead Sea waters are noisome," he said; "and I have been drinking of them by long draughts."

"Long draughts!" I answered, thinking to console him. "Draughts have not been long which can have been swallowed in your years. Your disease may be acute, but it cannot yet have become chronic. A man always thinks at the moment of each misfortune that that special misery will last his lifetime; but God is too good for that. I do not know what ails you; but this day twelvemonth will see you again as sound as a roach."

We then sat silent for a while, during which I was puffing at a cigar. Smith, among his accomplishments, did not reckon that of smoking,—which was a grief to me; for a man enjoys the tobacco doubly when another is enjoying it with him.

"No, you do not know what ails me," he said at last, "and, therefore, cannot judge."

"Perhaps not, my dear fellow. But my experience tells me that early wounds are generally capable of cure; and, therefore, I surmise that yours may be so. The heart at your time of life is not worn out, and has strength and soundness left wherewith to throw off its maladies. I hope it may be so with you."

"God knows. I do not mean to say that there are none more to be pitied than I am; but at the present moment, I am not—not light—hearted."

"I wish I could ease your burden, my dear fellow."

"It is most preposterous in me thus to force myself upon you, and then trouble you with my cares. But I had been alone so long, and I was so weary of it!"

"By Jove, and so had I. Make no apology. And let me tell you this,—though perhaps you will not credit me,—that I would sooner laugh with a comrade than cry with him is true enough; but, if occasion demands, I can do the latter also."

He then put out his hand to me, and I pressed it in token of my friendship. My own hand was hot and rough with the heat and sand; but his was soft and cool almost as a woman's. I thoroughly hate an effeminate man; but, in spite of a certain womanly softness about this fellow, I could not hate him. "Yes," I continued, "though somewhat unused to the melting mood, I also sometimes give forth my medicinal gums. I don't want to ask you any questions, and, as a rule, I hate to be told secrets, but if I can be of any service to you in any matter I will do my best. I don't say this with reference to the present moment, but think of it before we part."

I looked round at him and saw that he was in tears. "I know that you will think that I am a weak fool," he said, pressing his handkerchief to his eyes.

"By no means. There are moments in a man's life when it becomes him to weep like a woman; but the older he grows the more seldom those moments come to him. As far as I can see of men, they never cry at that which disgraces them."

"It is left for women to do that," he answered.

"Oh, women! A woman cries for everything and for nothing. It is the sharpest arrow she has in her quiver,—the best card in her hand. When a woman cries, what can you do but give her all she asks for?"

"Do you—dislike women?"

"No, by Jove! I am never really happy unless one is near me, or more than one. A man, as a rule, has an amount of energy within him which he cannot turn to profit on himself alone. It is good for him to have a woman by him that he may work for her, and thus have exercise for his limbs and faculties. I am very fond of women. But I always like those best who are most helpless."

We were silent again for a while, and it was during this time that I found myself lying with my head in his lap. I had slept, but it could have been but for a few minutes, and when I woke I found his hand upon my brow. As I started up he said that the flies had been annoying me, and that he had not chosen to waken me as I seemed weary. "It has been that double bathing," I said, apologetically; for I always feel ashamed when I am detected sleeping in the day. "In hot weather the water does make one drowsy. By Jove, it's getting dark; we had better have the horses."

"Stay half a moment," he said, speaking very softly, and laying his hand upon my arm, "I will not detain you a minute."

"There is no hurry in life," I said.

"You promised me just now you would assist me."

"If it be in my power, I will."

"Before we part at Alexandria I will endeavour to tell you the story of my troubles, and then if you can aid me—" It struck me as he paused that I had made a rash promise, but nevertheless I must stand by it now—with one or two provisoes. The chances were that the young man was short of money, or else that he had got into a scrape about a girl. In either ease I might give him some slight assistance; but, then, it behoved me to make him understand that I would not consent to become a participator in mischief. I was too old to get my head willingly into a scrape, and this I must endeavour to make him understand.

"I will, if it be in my power," I said. "I will ask no questions now; but if your trouble be about some lady—"

"It is not," said he.

"Well; so be it. Of all troubles those are the most troublesome. If you are short of cash—"

"No, I am not short of cash."

"You are not. That's well too; for want of money is a sore trouble also." And then I paused before I came to the point. "I do not suspect anything bad of you, Smith. Had I done so, I should not have spoken as I have done. And if there be nothing bad—"

"There is nothing disgraceful," he said.

"That is just what I mean; and in that case I will do anything for you that may be within my power. Now let us look for Joseph and the mucherry-boy, for it is time that we were at Jericho."

I cannot describe at length the whole of our journey from thence to our tents at Jericho, nor back to Jerusalem, nor even from Jerusalem to Jaffa. At Jericho we did sleep in tents, paying so much per night, according to the tariff. We wandered out at night, and drank coffee with a family of Arabs in the desert, sitting in a ring round their coffee-kettle. And we saw a Turkish soldier punished with the bastinado,—a sight which did not do me any good, and which made Smith very sick. Indeed after the first blow he walked away. Jericho is a remarkable spot in that pilgrim week, and I wish I had space to describe it. But I have not, for I must hurry on, back to Jerusalem and thence to Jaffa. I had much to tell also of those Bedouins; how they were essentially true to us, but teased us almost to frenzy by their continual begging. They begged for our food and our drink, for our cigars and our gunpowder, for the clothes off our backs, and the handkerchiefs out of our pockets. As to gunpowder I had none to give them, for my charges were all made up in cartridges; and I learned that the guns behind their backs were a mere pretence, for they had not a grain of powder among them.

We slept one night in Jerusalem, and started early on the following morning. Smith came to my hotel so that we might be ready together for the move. We still carried with us Joseph and the mucherry-boy; but for our Bedouins, who had duly received their forty shillings a piece, we had no further use. On our road down to Jerusalem we had much chat together, but only one adventure. Those pilgrims, of whom I have spoken, journey to Jerusalem in the greatest number by the route which we were now taking from it, and they come in long droves, reaching Jaffa in crowds by the French and Austrian steamers from Smyrna, Damascus, and Constantinople. As their number confers security in that somewhat insecure country, many travellers from the west of Europe make arrangements to travel with them. On our way down we met the last of these caravans for the year, and we were passing it for more than two hours. On this occasion I rode first, and Smith was immediately behind me; but of a sudden I observed him to wheel his horse round, and to clamber downwards among bushes and stones towards a river that ran below us. "Hallo, Smith," I cried, "you will destroy your horse, and yourself too." But he would not answer me, and all I could do was to draw up in the path and wait. My confusion was made the worse, as at that moment a long string of pilgrims was passing by. "Good morning, sir," said an old man to me in good English. I looked up as I answered him, and saw a grey—haired gentleman, of very solemn and sad aspect. He might be seventy years of age, and I could see that he was attended by three or four servants. I shall never forget the severe and sorrowful expression of his eyes, over which his heavy eyebrows hung low. "Are there many English in Jerusalem?" he asked. "A good many," I replied; "there always are at Easter." "Can you tell me anything of any of them?" he asked. "Not a word," said I, for I knew no one; "but our consul can." And then we bowed to each other and he passed on.

I got off my horse and scrambled down on foot after Smith. I found him gathering berries and bushes as though his very soul were mad with botany; but as I had seen nothing of this in him before, I asked what strange freak had taken him.

"You were talking to that old man," he said.

"Well, yes, I was."

"That is the relation of whom I have spoken to you."

"The d—he is!"

"And I would avoid him, if it be possible."

I then learned that the old gentleman was his uncle. He had no living father or mother, and he now supposed that his relative was going to Jerusalem in quest of him. "If so," said I, "you will undoubtedly give him leg bail, unless the Austrian boat is more than ordinarily late. It is as much as we shall do to catch it, and you may be half over Africa, or far gone on your way to India, before he can be on your track again."

"I will tell you all about it at Alexandria," he replied; and then he scrambled up again with his horse, and we went on. That night we slept at the Armenian convent at Ramlath, or Ramath. This place is supposed to stand on the site of Arimathea, and is marked as such in many of the maps. The monks at this time of the year are very busy, as the pilgrims all stay here for one night on their routes backwards and forwards, and the place on such occasions is terribly crowded. On the night of our visit it was nearly empty, as a caravan had left it that morning; and thus we were indulged with separate cells, a point on which my companion seemed to lay considerable stress.

On the following day, at about noon, we entered Jaffa, and put up at an inn there which is kept by a Pole. The boat from Beyrout, which touches at Jaffa on its way to Alexandria, was not yet in, nor even sighted; we were therefore amply in time. "Shall we sail to-night?" I asked of the agent. "Yes, in all probability," he replied. "If the signal be seen before three we shall do so. If not, then not;" and so I returned to the hotel.

Smith had involuntarily shown signs of fatigue during the journey, but yet he had borne up well against it. I had never felt called on to grant any extra indulgence as to time because the work was too much for him. But now he was a good deal knocked up, and I was a little frightened fearing that I had over-driven him under the heat of the sun. I was alarmed lest he should have fever, and proposed to send for the Jaffa doctor. But this he utterly refused. He would shut himself for an hour or two in his room, he said, and by that time he trusted the boat would be in sight. It was clear to me that he was very anxious on the subject, fearing that his uncle would be back upon his heels before he had started.

I ordered a serious breakfast for myself, for with me, on such occasions, my appetite demands more immediate attention than my limbs. I also acknowledge that

I become fatigued, and can lay myself at length during such idle days and sleep from hour to hour; but the desire to do so never comes till I have well eaten and drunken. A bottle of French wine, three or four cutlets of goats' flesh, an omelet made out of the freshest eggs, and an enormous dish of oranges, was the banquet set before me; and though I might have found fault with it in Paris or London, I thought that it did well enough in Jaffa. My poor friend could not join me, but had a cup of coffee in his room. "At any rate take a little brandy in it," I said to him, as I stood over his bed. "I could not swallow it," said he, looking at me with almost beseeching eyes. "Beshrew the fellow," I said to myself as I left him, carefully closing the door, so that the sound should not shake him; "he is little better than a woman, and yet I have become as fond of him as though he were my brother."

I went out at three, but up to that time the boat had not been signalled. "And we shall not get out to-night?" "No, not to-night," said the agent. "And what time to-morrow?" "If she comes in this evening, you will start by daylight. But they so manage her departure from Beyrout, that she seldom is here in the evening." "It will be noon to-morrow then?" "Yes," the man said, "noon to-morrow." I calculated, however, that the old gentleman could not possibly be on our track by that time. He would not have reached Jerusalem till late in the day on which we saw him, and it would take him some time to obtain tidings of his nephew. But it might be possible that messengers sent by him should reach Jaffa by four or five on the day after his arrival. That would be this very day which we were now wasting at Jaffa. Having thus made my calculations, I returned to Smith to give him such consolation as it might be in my power to afford.

He seemed to be dreadfully afflicted by all this. "He will have traced me to Jerusalem, and then again away; and will follow me immediately."

"That is all very well," I said; "but let even a young man do the best he can, and he will not get from Jerusalem to Jaffa in less than twelve hours. Your uncle is not a young man, and could not possibly do the journey under two days."

"But he will send. He will not mind what money he spends."

"And if he does send, take off your hat to his messengers, and bid them carry your complaints back. You are not a felon whom he can arrest."

"No, he cannot arrest me; but, ah! you do not understand;" and then he sat up on the bed, and seemed as though he were going to wring his hands in despair.

I waited for some half hour in his room, thinking that he would tell me this story of his. If he required that I should give him my aid in the presence either of his uncle or of his uncle's myrmidons, I must at any rate know what was likely to be the dispute between them. But as he said nothing I suggested that he should stroll out with me among the orange-groves by which the town is surrounded. In answer to this he looked up piteously into my face as though begging me to be merciful to him. "You are strong," said he, "and cannot understand what it is to feel fatigue as I do." And yet he had declared on commencing his journey that he would not be found to complain? Nor had he complained by a single word till after that encounter with his uncle. Nay, he had borne up well till this news had reached us of the boat being late. I felt convinced that if the boat were at this moment lying in the harbour all that appearance of excessive weakness would soon vanish. What it was that he feared I could not guess; but it was manifest to me that some great terror almost overwhelmed him.

"My idea is," said I, and I suppose that I spoke with something less of good-nature in my tone than I had assumed for the last day or two, "that no man should, under any circumstances, be so afraid of another man, as to tremble at his presence,—either at his presence or his expected presence."

"Ah, now you are angry with me; now you despise me!"

"Neither the one nor the other. But if I may take the liberty of a friend with you, I should advise you to combat this feeling of horror. If you do not, it will unman you. After all, what can your uncle do to you? He cannot rob you of your heart and soul. He cannot touch your inner self."

"You do not know," he said.

"Ah but, Smith, I do know that. Whatever may be this quarrel between you and him, you should not tremble at the thought of him; unless indeed—"

"Unless what?"

"Unless you had done aught that should make you tremble before every honest man." I own I had begun to have my doubts of him, and to fear that he had absolutely disgraced himself. Even in such case I,—I individually,—did not wish to be severe on him; but I should be annoyed to find that I had opened my heart to a swindler or a practised knave.

"I will tell you all to-morrow," said he; "but I have been guilty of nothing of that sort."

In the evening he did come out, and sat with me as I smoked my cigar. The boat, he was told, would almost undoubtedly come in by daybreak on the following morning, and be off at nine; whereas it was very improbable that any arrival from Jerusalem would be so early as that. "Beside," I reminded him, "your uncle will hardly hurry down to Jaffa, because he will have no reason to think but what you have already started. There are no telegraphs here, you know."

In the evening he was still very sad, though the paroxysm of his terror seemed to have passed away. I would not bother him, as he had himself chosen the following morning for the telling of his story. So I sat and smoked, and talked to him about our past journey, and by degrees the power of speech came back to him, and I again felt that I loved him! Yes, loved him! I have not taken many such fancies into my head, at so short a notice; but I did love him, as though he were a younger brother. I felt a delight in serving him, and though I was almost old enough to be his father, I ministered to him as though he had been an old man, or a woman.

On the following morning we were stirring at daybreak, and found that the vessel was in sight. She would be in the roads off the town in two hours' time, they said, and would start at eleven or twelve. And then we walked round by the gate of the town, and sauntered a quarter of a mile or so along the way that leads towards Jerusalem. I could see that his eye was anxiously turned down the road, but he said nothing. We saw no cloud of dust, and then we returned to breakfast.

"The steamer has come to anchor," said our dirty Polish host to us in execrable English. "And we may be off on board," said Smith. "Not yet," he said; "they must put their cargo out first." I saw, however, that Smith was uneasy, and I made up my mind to go off to the vessel at once. When they should see an English portmanteau making an offer to come up the gangway, the Austrian sailors would not stop it. So I called for the bill, and ordered that the things should be taken down to the wretched broken heap of rotten timber which they called a quay. Smith had not told me his story, but no doubt he would as soon as he was on board.

I was in the act of squabbling with the Pole over the last demand for piastres, when we heard a noise in the gateway of the inn, and I saw Smith's countenance become pale. It was an Englishman's voice asking if there were any strangers there; so I went into the courtyard, closing the door behind me, and turning the key upon the landlord and Smith. "Smith," said I to myself, "will keep the Pole quiet if he have any wit left."

The man who had asked the question had the air of an upper English servant, and I thought that I recognised one of those whom I had seen with the old gentleman on the road; but the matter was soon put at rest by the appearance of that gentleman himself. He walked up into the courtyard, looked hard at me from under those bushy eyebrows, just raised his hat, and then—said, "I believe I am speaking to Mr. Jones."

"Yes," said I, "I am Mr. Jones. Can I have the honour of serving you?"

There was something peculiarly unpleasant about this man's face. At the present moment I examined it closely, and could understand the great aversion which his nephew felt towards him. He looked like a gentleman and like a man of talent, nor was there anything of meanness in his face; neither was he ill-looking, in the usual acceptation of the word; but one could see that he was solemn, austere, and overbearing; that he would be incapable of any light enjoyment, and unforgiving towards all offences. I took him to be a man who, being old himself, could never remember that he had been young, and who, therefore, hated the levities of youth. To me such a character is specially odious; for I would fain, if it be possible, be young even to my grave. Smith, if he were clever, might escape from the window of the room, which opened out upon a terrace, and still get down to the steamer. I would keep the old man in play for some time; and, even though I lost my passage, would be true to my friend. There lay our joint luggage at my feet in the yard. If Smith would venture away without his portion of it, all might yet be right.

"My name, sir, is Sir William Weston," he began. I had heard of the name before, and knew him to be a man of wealth, and family, and note. I took off my hat, and said that I had much honour in meeting Sir William Weston.

"And I presume you know the object with which I am now here," he continued.

"Not exactly," said I. "Nor do I understand how I possibly should know it, seeing that, up to this moment, I did not even know your name, and have heard nothing concerning either your movements or your affairs."

"Sir," said he, "I have hitherto believed that I might at any rate expect from you the truth."

"Sir," said I, "I am bold to think that you will not dare to tell me, either now, or at any other time, that you have received, or expect to receive, from me anything that is not true."

He then stood still, looking at me for a moment or two, and I beg to assert that I looked as fully at him. There was, at any rate, no cause why I should tremble before him. I was not his nephew, nor was I responsible for his nephew's doings towards him. Two of his servants were behind him, and on my side there stood a boy and girl belonging to the inn. They, however, could not understand a word of English. I saw that he was hesitating, but at last he spoke out. I confess, now, that his words, when they were spoken, did, at the first moment, make me tremble.

"I have to charge you," said he, "with eloping with my niece, and I demand of you to inform me where she is. You are perfectly aware that I am her guardian by law."

I did tremble;—not that I cared much for Sir William's guardianship, but I saw before me so terrible an embarrassment! And then I felt so thoroughly abashed in that I had allowed myself to be so deceived! It all came back upon me in a moment, and covered me with a shame that even made me blush. I had travelled through the desert with a woman for days, and had not discovered her, though she had given me a thousand signs. All those signs I remembered now, and I blushed painfully. When her hand was on my forehead I still thought that she was a man! I declare that at this moment I felt a stronger disinclination to face my late companion than I did to encounter her angry uncle.

"Your niece!" I said, speaking with a sheepish bewilderment which should have convinced him at once of my innocence. She had asked me, too, whether I was a married man, and I had denied it. How was I to escape from such a mess of misfortunes? I declare that I began to forget her troubles in my own.

"Yes, my niece,—Miss Julia Weston. The disgrace which you have brought upon me must be wiped out; but my first duty is to save that unfortunate young woman from further misery."

"If it be as you say," I exclaimed, "by the honour of a gentleman—"

"I care nothing for the honour of a gentleman till I see it proved. Be good enough to inform me, sir, whether Miss Weston is in this house."

For a moment I hesitated; but I saw at once that I should make myself responsible for certain mischief, of which I was at any rate hitherto in truth innocent, if I allowed myself to become a party to concealing a young lady. Up to this period I could at any rate defend myself, whether my defence were believed or not believed. I still had a hope that the charming Julia might have escaped through the window, and a feeling that if she had done so I was not responsible. When I turned the lock I turned it on Smith.

For a moment I hesitated, and then walked slowly across the yard and opened the door. "Sir William," I said, as I did so, "I travelled here with a companion dressed as a man; and I believed him to be what he seemed till this minute."

"Sir!" said Sir William, with a look of scorn in his face which gave me the lie in my teeth as plainly as any words could do. And then he entered the room. The Pole was standing in one corner, apparently amazed at what was going on, and Smith,—I may as well call her Miss Weston at once, for the baronet's statement was true,—was sitting on a sort of divan in the corner of the chamber hiding her face in her hands. She had made no attempt at an escape, and a full explanation was therefore indispensable. For myself I own that I felt ashamed of my part in the play,—ashamed even of my own innocency. Had I been less innocent I should certainly have contrived to appear much less guilty. Had it occurred to me on the banks of the Jordan that Smith was a lady, I should not have travelled with her in her gentleman's habiliments from Jerusalem to Jaffa. Had she consented to remain under my protection, she must have done so without a masquerade.

The uncle stood still and looked at his niece. He probably understood how thoroughly stern and disagreeable was his own face, and considered that he could punish the crime of his relative in no severer way than by looking at her. In this I think he was right. But at last there was a necessity for speaking. "Unfortunate young woman!" he said, and then paused.

"We had better get rid of the landlord," I said, "before we come to any explanation." And I motioned to the man to leave the room. This he did very unwillingly, but at last he was gone.

"I fear that it is needless to care on her account who may hear the story of her shame," said Sir William. I looked at Miss Weston, but she still sat hiding her face. However, if she did not defend herself, it was necessary that I should defend both her and me.

"I do not know how far I may be at liberty to speak with reference to the private matters of yourself or of your—your niece, Sir William Weston. I would not willingly interfere—"

"Sir," said he, "your interference has already taken place. Will you have the goodness to explain to me what are your intentions with regard to that lady?"

My intentions! Heaven help me! My intentions, of course, were to leave her in her uncle's hands. Indeed,

I could hardly be said to have formed any intention since I had learned that I had been honoured by a lady's presence. At this moment I deeply regretted that I had thoughtlessly stated to her that I was an unmarried man. In doing so I had had no object. But at that time "Smith" had been quite a stranger to me, and I had not thought it necessary to declare my own private concerns. Since that I had talked so little of myself that the fact of my family at home had not been mentioned. "Will you have the goodness to explain what are your intentions with regard to that lady?" said the baronet.

"Oh, Uncle William!" exclaimed Miss Weston, now at length raising her head from her hands.

"Hold your peace, madam," said he. "When called upon to speak, you will find your words with difficulty enough. Sir, I am waiting for an answer from you."

"But, uncle, he is nothing to me;—the gentleman is nothing to me!"

"By the heavens above us, he shall be something, or I will know the reason why! What! he has gone off with you; he has travelled through the country with you, hiding you from your only natural friend; he has been your companion for weeks—"

"Six days, sir," said I.

"Sir!" said the baronet, again giving me the lie. "And now," he continued, addressing his niece, "you tell me that he is nothing to you. He shall give me his promise that he will make you his wife at the consulate at Alexandria, or I will destroy him. I know who he is."

"If you know who I am," said I, "you must know—"

But he would not listen to me. "And as for you, mad-am, unless he makes me that promise—" And then he paused in his threat, and, turning round, looked me in the face. I saw that she also was looking at me, though not openly as he did; and some flattering devil that was at work round my heart, would have persuaded that she also would have heard a certain answer given without dismay,—would even have re-ceived comfort in her agony from such an answer. But the reader knows how completely that answer was out of my power.

"I have not the slightest ground for supposing," said I, "that the lady would accede to such an arrangement,—if it were possible. My acquaintance with her has been altogether confined to—. To tell the truth, I have not been in Miss Weston's confidence, and have only taken her for that which she has seemed to be."

"Sir!" said the baronet, again looking at me as though he would wither me on the spot for my falsehood.

"It is true!" said Julia, getting up from her seat, and appealing with clasped hands to her uncle—"as true as Heaven."

"Madam!" said he, "do you both take me for a fool?"

"That you should take me for one," said I, "would be very natural. The facts are as we state to you. Miss Weston,—as I now learn that she is,—did me the hon-our of calling at my hotel, having heard—" And then it seemed to me as though I were attempting to screen myself by telling the story against her, so I was again silent. Never in my life had I been in a position of such extraordinary difficulty. The duty which I owed to Ju-lia as a woman, and to Sir William as a guardian, and to myself as the father of a family, all clashed with each other. I was anxious to be generous, honest, and prudent, but it was impossible; so I made up my mind to say nothing further.

"Mr. Jones," said the baronet, "I have explained to you the only arrangement which under the present circumstances I can permit to pass without open exposure and condign punishment. That you are a gentleman by birth, education, and position I am aware,"—whereupon I raised my hat, and then he continued: "That lady has three hundred a year of her own—"

"And attractions, personal and mental, which are worth ten times the money," said I, and I bowed to my fair friend, who looked at me the while with sad beseeching eyes. I confess that the mistress of my bosom, had she known my thoughts at that one moment, might have had cause for anger.

"Very well," continued he. "Then the proposal which I name, cannot, I imagine, but be satisfactory. If you will make to her and to me the only amends which it is in your power as a gentleman to afford, I will forgive all. Tell me that you will make her your wife on your arrival in Egypt."

I would have given anything not to have looked at Miss Weston at this moment, but I could not help it. I did turn my face half round to her before I answered, and then felt that I had been cruel in doing so. "Sir William," said I, "I have at home already a wife and family of my own."

"It is not true!" said he, retreating a step, and staring at me with amazement.

"There is something, sir," I replied, "in the unprecedented circumstances of this meeting, and in your position with regard to that lady, which, joined to your advanced age, will enable me to regard that useless insult as unspoken. I am a married man. There is the signature of my wife's last letter," and I handed him one which I had received as I was leaving Jerusalem.

But the coarse violent contradiction which Sir William had given me was nothing compared with the reproach conveyed in Miss Weston's countenance. She looked at me as though all her anger were now turned against me. And yet, methought, there was more of sorrow than of resentment in her countenance. But what cause was there for either? Why should I be reproached, even by her look? She did not remember at the moment that when I answered her chance question as to my domestic affairs, I had answered it as to a man who was a stranger to me, and not as to a beautiful woman, with whom I was about to pass certain days in close and intimate society. To her, at the moment, it seemed as though I had cruelly deceived her. In truth, the one person really deceived had been myself.

And here I must explain, on behalf of the lady, that when she first joined me she had no other view than that of seeing the banks of the Jordan in that guise which she had chosen to assume, in order to escape from the solemnity and austerity of a disagreeable relative. She had been very foolish, and that was all. I take it that she had first left her uncle at Constantinople, but on this point I never got certain information. Afterwards, while we were travelling together, the idea had come upon her, that she might go on as far as Alexandria with me. And then I know nothing further of the lady's intentions, but I am certain that her wishes were good and pure. Her uncle had been intolerable to her, and she had fled from him. Such had been her offence, and no more.

"Then, sir," said the baronet, giving me back my letter, "you must be a double-dyed villain."

"And you, sir," said I—. But here Julia Weston interrupted me.

"Uncle, you altogether wrong this gentleman," she said. "He has been kind to me beyond my power of words to express; but, till told by you, he knew nothing of my secret. Nor would he have known it," she added, looking down upon the ground. As to that latter assertion, I was at liberty to believe as much as I pleased.

The Pole now came to the door, informing us that any who wished to start by the packet must go on board, and therefore, as the unreasonable old gentleman perceived, it was necessary that we should all make our arrangements. I cannot say that they were such as enable me to look back on them with satisfaction. He did seem now at last to believe that I had been an unconscious agent in his niece's stratagem, but he hardly on that account became civil to me. "It was absolutely necessary," he said, "that he and that unfortunate young woman," as he would call her, "should depart at once,—by this ship now going." To this proposition of course I made no opposition. "And you, Mr. Jones," he continued, "will at once perceive that you, as a gentleman, should allow us to proceed on our journey without the honour of your company."

This was very dreadful, but what could I say; or, indeed, what could I do? My most earnest desire in the matter was to save Miss Weston from annoyance; and under existing circumstances my presence on board could not but be a burden to her. And then, if I went,—if I did go, in opposition to the wishes of the baronet, could I trust my own prudence? It was better for all parties that I should remain.

"Sir William," said I, after a minute's consideration, "if you will apologise to me for the gross insults you have offered me, it shall be as you say."

"Mr. Jones," said Sir William, "I do apologise for the words which I used to you while I was labouring under a very natural misconception of the circumstances." I do not know that I was much the better for the apology, but at the moment I regarded it sufficient.

Their things were then hurried down to the strand, and I accompanied them to the ruined quay. I took off my hat to Sir William as he was first let down into the boat. He descended first, so that he might receive his niece,—for all Jaffa now knew that it was a lady,—and then I gave her my hand for the last time. "God bless you, Miss Weston," I said, pressing it closely. "God bless you, Mr. Jones," she replied. And from that day to this I have neither spoken to her nor seen her.

I waited a fortnight at Jaffa for the French boat, eating cutlets of goat's flesh, and wandering among the orange groves. I certainly look back on that fortnight as the most miserable period of my life. I had been deceived, and had failed to discover the deceit, even though the deceiver had perhaps wished that I should do so. For that blindness I have never forgiven myself.

An Unprotected Female
at the Pyramids

I n the happy days when we were young, no description conveyed to us so complete an idea of mysterious reality as that of an Oriental city. We knew it was actually there, but had such vague notions of its ways and looks! Let any one remember his early impressions as to Bagdad or Grand Cairo, and then say if this was not so. It was probably taken from the "Arabian Nights," and the picture produced was one of strange, fantastic, luxurious houses; of women who were either very young and very beautiful, or else very old and very cunning; but in either state exercising much more influence in life than women in the East do now; of good-natured, capricious, though sometimes tyrannical monarchs; and of life full of quaint mysteries, quite unintelligible in every phasis, and on that account the more picturesque.

And perhaps Grand Cairo has thus filled us with more wonder even than Bagdad. We have been in a certain manner at home at Bagdad, but have only visited Grand Cairo occasionally. I know no place which was to me, in early years, so delightfully mysterious as Grand Cairo.

But the route to India and Australia has changed all this. Men from all countries going to the East, now pass through Cairo, and its streets and costumes are no longer strange to us. It has become also a resort for invalids, or rather for those who fear that they may become invalids if they remain in a cold climate during the winter months. And thus at Cairo there is always to be found a considerable population of French, Americans, and of English. Oriental life is brought home to us, dreadfully diluted by western customs, and the delights of the "Arabian Nights" are shorn of half their value. When we have seen a thing it is never so magnificent to us as when it was half unknown.

It is not much that we deign to learn from these Orientals,—we who glory in our civilisation. We do not copy their silence or their abstemiousness, nor that invariable mindfulness of his own personal dignity which always adheres to a Turk or to an Arab. We chatter as much at Cairo as elsewhere, and eat as much and drink as much, and dress ourselves generally in the same old ugly costume. But we do usually take upon ourselves to wear red caps, and we do ride on donkeys.

Nor are the visitors from the West to Cairo by any means confined to the male sex. Ladies are to be seen in the streets quite regardless of the Mahommedan custom which presumes a veil to be necessary for an appearance in public; and, to tell the truth, the Mahommedans in general do not appear to be much shocked by their effrontery.

A quarter of the town has in this way become inhabited by men wearing coats and waistcoats, and by women who are without veils; but the English tongue in Egypt finds its centre at Shepheard's Hotel. It is here that people congregate who are looking out for parties to visit with them the Upper Nile, and who are generally all smiles and courtesy; and here also are to be found they who have just returned from this journey, and who are often in a frame of mind towards their companions that is much less amiable. From hence, during the winter, a cortege proceeds almost daily to the pyramids, or to Memphis, or to the petrified forest, or to the City of the Sun. And then, again, four or five times a month the house is filled with young aspirants going out to India, male and female, full of valour and bloom; or with others coming home, no longer young, no longer aspiring, but laden with children and grievances.

The party with whom we are at present concerned is not about to proceed further than the Pyramids, and we shall be able to go with them and return in one and the same day.

It consisted chiefly of an English family, Mr. and Mrs. Damer, their daughter, and two young sons;— of these chiefly, because they were the nucleus to which the others had attached themselves as adherents; they had originated the journey, and in the whole management of it Mr. Damer retarded himself as the master.

The adherents were, firstly, M. Delabordeau, a Frenchman, now resident in Cairo, who had given out that he was in some way concerned in the canal about to be made between the Mediterranean and the Red Sea. In discussion on this subject he had become acquainted with Mr. Damer; and although the latter gentleman, true to English interests, perpetually declared that the canal would never be made, and thus irritated M. Delabordeau not a little—nevertheless, some measure of friendship had grown up between them.

There was also an American gentleman, Mr. Jefferson Ingram, who was comprising all countries and all nations in one grand tour, as American gentlemen so often do. He was young and good-looking, and had made himself especially agreeable to Mr. Damer, who had declared, more than once, that Mr. Ingram was by far the most rational American he had ever met. Mr. Ingram would listen to Mr. Damer by the half-hour as to the virtue of the British Constitution, and had even sat by almost with patience when Mr. Damer had expressed a doubt as to the good working of the United States' scheme of policy,—which, in an American, was most wonderful. But some of the sojourners at Shepheard's had observed that Mr. Ingram was in the habit of talking with Miss Damer almost as much as with her father, and argued from that, that fond as the young man was of politics, he did sometimes turn his mind to other things also.

And then there was Miss Dawkins. Now Miss Dawkins was an important person, both as to herself and as to her line of life, and she must be described. She was, in the first place, an unprotected female of about thirty years of age. As this is becoming an established profession, setting itself up as it were in opposition to the old world idea that women, like green peas, cannot come to perfection without supporting-sticks, it will be understood at once what were Miss Dawkins's sentiments. She considered—or at any rate so expressed herself— that peas could grow very well without sticks, and could not only grow thus unsupported, but could also make their way about the world without any incumbrance of sticks whatsoever. She did not intend, she said, to rival Ida Pfeiffer, seeing that she was attached in a moderate way to bed and board, and was attached to society in a manner almost more than moderate; but she had no idea of being prevented from seeing anything she wished to see because she had neither father, nor husband, nor brother available for the purpose of escort. She was a human creature, with arms and legs, she said; and she intended to use them. And this was all very well; but nevertheless she had a strong inclination to use the arms and legs of other people when she could make them serviceable.

In person Miss Dawkins was not without attraction. I should exaggerate if I were to say that she was beautiful and elegant; but she was good looking, and not usually ill mannered. She was tall, and gifted with features rather sharp and with eyes very bright. Her hair was of the darkest shade of brown, and was always worn in bandeaux, very neatly. She appeared generally in black, though other circumstances did not lead one to suppose that she was in mourning; and then, no other travelling costume is so convenient! She always wore a dark broad—brimmed straw hat, as to the ribbons on which she was rather particular. She was very neat about her gloves and boots; and though it cannot be said that her dress was got up without reference to expense, there can be no doubt that it was not effected without considerable outlay,—and more considerable thought.

Miss Dawkins—Sabrina Dawkins was her name, but she seldom had friends about her intimate enough to use the word Sabrina—was certainly a clever young woman. She could talk on most subjects, if not well, at least well enough to amuse. If she had not read much, she never showed any lamentable deficiency; she was good-humoured, as a rule, and could on occasions be very soft and winning. People who had known her long would sometimes say that she was selfish; but with new acquaintance she was forbearing and self-denying.

With what income Miss Dawkins was blessed no one seemed to know. She lived like a gentlewoman, as far as outward appearance went, and never seemed to be in want; but some people would say that she knew very well how many sides there were to a shilling, and some enemy had once declared that she was an "old soldier." Such was Miss Dawkins.

She also, as well as Mr. Ingram and M. Delabordeau, had laid herself out to find the weak side of Mr. Damer. Mr. Damer, with all his family, was going up the Nile, and it was known that he had room for two in his boat over and above his own family. Miss Dawkins had told him that she had not quite made up her mind to undergo so great a fatigue, but that, nevertheless, she had a longing of the soul to see something of Nubia. To this Mr. Damer had answered nothing but "Oh!" which Miss Dawkins had not found to be encouraging.

But she had not on that account despaired. To a married man there are always two sides, and in this instance there was Mrs. Damer as well as Mr. Damer. When Mr. Damer said "Oh!" Miss Dawkins sighed, and said, "Yes, indeed!" then smiled, and betook herself to Mrs. Damer.

Now Mrs. Damer was soft-hearted, and also somewhat old-fashioned. She did not conceive any violent affection for Miss Dawkins, but she told her daughter that "the single lady by herself was a very nice young woman, and that it was a thousand pities she should have to go about so much alone like."

Miss Damer had turned up her pretty nose, thinking, perhaps, how small was the chance that it ever should be her own lot to be an unprotected female. But Miss

Dawkins carried her point at any rate as regarded the expedition to the Pyramids.

Miss Damer, I have said, had a pretty nose. I may also say that she had pretty eyes, mouth, and chin, with other necessary appendages, all pretty. As to the two Master Damers, who were respectively of the ages of fifteen and sixteen, it may be sufficient to say that they were conspicuous for red caps and for the constancy with which they raced their donkeys.

And now the donkeys, and the donkey boys, and the dragomans were all standing at the steps of Shepheard's Hotel. To each donkey there was a donkey-boy, and to each gentleman there was a dragoman, so that a goodly cortege was assembled, and a goodly noise was made. It may here be remarked, perhaps with some little pride, that not half the noise is given in Egypt to persons speaking any other language that is bestowed on those whose vocabulary is English.

This lasted for half an hour. Had the party been French the donkeys would have arrived only fifteen minutes before the appointed time. And then out came Damer pere and Damer mere, Damer fille, and Damer fils. Damer mere was leaning on her husband, as was her wont. She was not an unprotected female, and had no desire to make any attempts in that line. Damer fille was attended sedulously by Mr. Ingram, for whose demolishment, however, Mr. Damer still brought up, in a loud voice, the fag ends of certain political arguments which he would fain have poured direct into the ears of his opponent, had not his wife been so persistent in claiming her privileges. M. Delabordeau should have followed with Miss Dawkins, but his French politeness, or else his fear of the unprotected female, taught him to walk on the other side of the mistress of the party.

Miss Dawkins left the house with an eager young Damer yelling on each side of her; but nevertheless, though thus neglected by the gentlemen of the party, she was all smiles and prettiness, and looked so sweetly on Mr. Ingram when that gentleman stayed a moment to help her on to her donkey, that his heart almost misgave him for leaving her as soon as she was in her seat.

And then they were off. In going from the hotel to the Pyramids our party had not to pass through any of the queer old narrow streets of the true Cairo—Cairo the Oriental. They all lay behind them as they went down by the back of the hotel, by the barracks of the Pasha and the College of the Dervishes, to the village of old Cairo and the banks of the Nile.

Here they were kept half an hour while their dragomans made a bargain with the ferryman, a stately reis, or captain of a boat, who declared with much dignity that he could not carry them over for a sum less than six times the amount to which he was justly entitled; while the dragomans, with great energy on behalf of their masters, offered him only five times that sum.

As far as the reis was concerned, the contest might soon have been at an end, for the man was not without a conscience; and would have been content with five times and a half; but then the three dragomans quarrelled among themselves as to which should have the paying of the money, and the affair became very tedious.

"What horrid, odious men!" said Miss Dawkins, appealing to Mr. Damer. "Do you think they will let us go over at all?"

"Well, I suppose they will; people do get over generally, I believe. Abdallah! Abdallah! why don't you pay the man? That fellow is always striving to save half a pias-tre for me."

"I wish he wasn't quite so particular," said Mrs. Damer, who was already becoming rather tired; "but I'm sure he's a very honest man in trying to protect us from be-ing robbed."

"That he is," said Miss Dawkins. "What a delightful trait of national character it is to see these men so faithful to their employers." And then at last they got over the ferry, Mr. Ingram having descended among the com-batants, and settled the matter in dispute by threats and shouts, and an uplifted stick.

They crossed the broad Nile exactly at the spot where the nilometer, or river guage, measures from day to day, and from year to year, the increasing or decreas-ing treasures of the stream, and landed at a village where thousands of eggs are made into chickens by the process of artificial incubation.

Mrs. Damer thought that it was very hard upon the maternal hens—the hens which should have been ma-ternal—that they should be thus robbed of the delights of motherhood.

"So unnatural, you know," said Miss Dawkins; "so op-posed to the fostering principles of creation. Don't you think so, Mr. Ingram?"

Mr. Ingram said he didn't know. He was again seating Miss Damer on her donkey, and it must be presumed that he performed this feat clumsily; for Fanny Damer could jump on and off the animal with hardly a fin-ger to help her, when her brother or her father was her escort; but now, under the hands of Mr. Ingram, this work of mounting was one which required considerable time and care. All which Miss Dawkins observed with precision.

"It's all very well talking," said Mr. Damer, bringing up his donkey nearly alongside that of Mr. Ingram, and ignoring his daughter's presence, just as he would have done that of his dog; "but you must admit that political power is more equally distributed in England than it is in America."

"Perhaps it is," said Mr. Ingram; "equally distributed among, we will say, three dozen families," and he made a feint as though to hold in his impetuous donkey, using the spur, however, at the same time on the side that was unseen by Mr. Damer. As he did so, Fanny's donkey became equally impetuous, and the two cantered on in advance of the whole party. It was quite in vain that Mr. Damer, at the top of his voice, shouted out something about "three dozen corruptible demagogues." Mr. Ingram found it quite impossible to restrain his donkey so as to listen to the sarcasm.

"I do believe papa would talk politics," said Fanny, "if he were at the top of Mont Blanc, or under the Falls of Niagara. I do hate politics, Mr. Ingram."

"I am sorry for that, very," said Mr. Ingram, almost sadly.

"Sorry, why? You don't want me to talk politics, do you?"

"In America we are all politicians, more or less; and, therefore, I suppose you will hate us all."

"Well, I rather think I should," said Fanny; "you would be such bores." But there was something in her eye, as she spoke, which atoned for the harshness of her words.

"A very nice young man is Mr. Ingram; don't you think so?" said Miss Dawkins to Mrs. Damer. Mrs. Damer was going along upon her donkey, not altogether comfortably. She much wished to have her lord and legitimate protector by her side, but he had left her to the care of a dragoman whose English was not intelligible to her, and she was rather cross.

"Indeed, Miss Dawkins, I don't know who are nice and who are not. This nasty donkey stumbles at ever step. There! I know I shall be down directly."

"You need not be at all afraid of that; they are perfectly safe, I believe, always," said Miss Dawkins, rising in her stirrup, and handling her reins quite triumphantly. "A very little practice will make you quite at home."

"I don't know what you mean by a very little practice. I have been here six weeks. Why did you put me on such a bad donkey as this?" and she turned to Abdallah, the dragoman.

"Him berry good donkey, my lady; berry good,—best of all. Call him Jack in Cairo. Him go to Pyramid and back, and mind noting."

"What does he say, Miss Dawkins?"

"He says that that donkey is one called Jack. If so I've had him myself many times, and Jack is a very good donkey."

"I wish you had him now with all my heart," said Mrs. Damer. Upon which Miss Dawkins offered to change; but those perils of mounting and dismounting were to Mrs. Damer a great deal too severe to admit of this.

"Seven miles of canal to be carried out into the sea, at a minimum depth of twenty-three feet, and the stone to be fetched from Heaven knows where! All the money in France wouldn't do it." This was addressed by Mr.

Damer to M. Delabordeau, whom he had caught after the abrupt flight of Mr. Ingram.

"Den we will borrow a leetle from England," said M. Delabordeau.

"Precious little, I can tell you. Such stock would not hold its price in our markets for twenty-four hours. If it were made, the freights would be too heavy to allow of merchandise passing through. The heavy goods would all go round; and as for passengers and mails, you don't expect to get them, I suppose, while there is a railroad ready made to their hand?"

"Ye vill carry all your ships through vidout any transportation. Think of that, my friend."

"Pshaw! You are worse than Ingram. Of all the plans I ever heard of it is the most monstrous, the most impracticable, the most—" But here he was interrupted by the entreaties of his wife, who had, in absolute deed and fact, slipped from her donkey, and was now calling lustily for her husband's aid. Whereupon Miss Dawkins allied herself to the Frenchman, and listened with an air of strong conviction to those arguments which were so weak in the ears of Mr. Damer. M. Delabordeau was about to ride across the Great Desert to Jerusalem, and it might perhaps be quite as well to do that with him, as to go up the Nile as far as the second cataract with the Damers.

"And so, M. Delabordeau, you intend really to start for Mount Sinai?"

"Yes, mees; ve intend to make one start on Monday week."

"And so on to Jerusalem. You are quite right. It would be a thousand pities to be in these countries, and to return without going over such ground as that. I shall certainly go to Jerusalem myself by that route."

"Vot, mees! you? Would you not find it too much fatigante?"

"I care nothing for fatigue, if I like the party I am with,—nothing at all, literally. You will hardly understand me, perhaps, M. Delabordeau; but I do not see any reason why I, as a young woman, should not make any journey that is practicable for a young man."

"Ah! dat is great resolution for you, mees."

"I mean as far as fatigue is concerned. You are a Frenchman, and belong to the nation that is at the head of all human civilisation—"

M. Delabordeau took off his hat and bowed low, to the peak of his donkey saddle. He dearly loved to hear his country praised, as Miss Dawkins was aware.

"And I am sure you must agree with me," continued Miss Dawkins, "that the time is gone by for women to consider themselves helpless animals, or to be so considered by others."

"Mees Dawkins vould never be considered, not in any times at all, to be one helpless animal," said M. Delabordeau civilly.

"I do not, at any rate, intend to be so regarded," said she. "It suits me to travel alone; not that I am averse to society; quite the contrary; if I meet pleasant people I am always ready to join them. But it suits me to travel without any permanent party, and I do not see why false shame should prevent my seeing the world as thoroughly as though I belonged to the other sex. Why should it, M. Delabordeau?"

M. Delabordeau declared that he did not see any reason why it should.

"I am passionately anxious to stand upon Mount Sinai," continued Miss Dawkins; "to press with my feet the earliest spot in sacred history, of the identity of which we are certain; to feel within me the awe-inspiring thrill of that thrice sacred hour!"

The Frenchman looked as though he did not quite understand her, but he said that it would be magnifique.

"You have already made up your party I suppose, M. Delabordeau?"

M. Delabordeau gave the names of two Frenchmen and one Englishman who were going with him.

"Upon my word it is a great temptation to join you," said Miss Dawkins, "only for that horrid Englishman."

"Vat, Mr. Stanley?"

"Oh, I don't mean any disrespect to Mr. Stanley. The horridness I speak of does not attach to him personally, but to his stiff, respectable, ungainly, well-behaved, irrational, and uncivilised country. You see I am not very patriotic."

"Not quite so much as my friend, Mr. Damer."

"Ha! ha! ha! an excellent creature, isn't he? And so they all are, dear creatures. But then they are so backward. They are most anxious that I should join them up the Nile, but—," and then Miss Dawkins shrugged her shoulders gracefully, and, as she flattered herself, like a Frenchwoman. After that they rode on in silence for a few moments.

"Yes, I must see Mount Sinai," said Miss Dawkins, and then sighed deeply. M. Delabordeau, notwithstanding that his country does stand at the head of all human civilisation, was not courteous enough to declare that if Miss Dawkins would join his party across the desert, nothing would be wanting to make his beatitude in this world perfect.

Their road from the village of the chicken-batching ovens lay up along the left bank of the Nile, through an immense grove of lofty palm—trees, looking out from among which our visitors could ever and anon see the heads of the two great Pyramids;—that is, such of them could see it as felt any solicitude in the matter.

It is astonishing how such things lose their great charm as men find themselves in their close neighbourhood. To one living in New York or London, how ecstatic is the interest inspired by these huge structures. One feels that no price would be too high to pay for seeing them as long as time and distance, and the world's inexorable task-work, forbid such a visit. How intense would be the delight of climbing over the wondrous handiwork of those wondrous architects so long since dead; how thrilling the awe with which one would penetrate down into their interior caves—those caves in which lay buried the bones of ancient kings, whose very names seem to have come to us almost from another world!

But all these feelings become strangely dim, their acute edges wonderfully worn, as the subjects which inspired them are brought near to us. "Ah! so those are the Pyramids, are they?" says the traveller, when the first glimpse of them is shown to him from the window of a railway carriage. "Dear me; they don't look so very high, do they? For Heaven's sake put the blind down, or we shall be destroyed by the dust." And then the ecstasy and keen delight of the Pyramids has vanished for ever.

Our friends, therefore, who for weeks past had seen from a distance, though they had not yet visited them, did not seem to have any strong feeling on the subject as they trotted through the grove of palm-trees. Mr. Damer had not yet escaped from his wife, who was still fretful from the result of her little accident.

"It was all the chattering of that Miss Dawkins," said Mrs. Damer. "She would not let me attend to what I was doing."

"Miss Dawkins is an ass," said her husband.

"It is a pity she has no one to look after her," said Mrs. Damer. M. Delabordeau was still listening to Miss Dawkins's raptures about Mount Sinai. "I wonder whether she has got any money," said M. Delabordeau to himself. "It can't be much," he went on thinking, "or she would not be left in this way by herself." And the result of his thoughts was that Miss Dawkins, if undertaken, might probably become more plague than profit. As to Miss Dawkins herself, though she was ecstatic about Mount Sinai—which was not present—she seemed to have forgotten the poor Pyramids, which were then before her nose.

The two lads were riding races along the dusty path, much to the disgust of their donkey-boys. Their time for enjoyment was to come. There were hampers to be opened; and then the absolute climbing of the Pyramids would actually be a delight to them.

As for Miss Damer and Mr. Ingram, it was clear that they had forgotten palm-trees, Pyramids, the Nile, and all Egypt. They had escaped to a much fairer paradise.

"Could I bear to live among Republicans?" said Fanny, repeating the last words of her American lover, and looking down from her donkey to the ground as she did so. "I hardly know what Republicans are, Mr. Ingram."

"Let me teach you," said he.

"You do talk such nonsense. I declare there is that Miss Dawkins looking at us as though she had twenty eyes. Could you not teach her, Mr. Ingram?"

And so they emerged from the palm-tree grove, through a village crowded with dirty, straggling Arab children, on to the cultivated plain, beyond which the Pyramids stood, now full before them; the two large Pyramids, a smaller one, and the huge sphynx's head all in a group together.

"Fanny," said Bob Damer, riding up to her, "mamma wants you; so toddle back."

"Mamma wants me! What can she want me for now?" said Fanny, with a look of anything but filial duty in her face.

"To protect her from Miss Dawkins, I think. She wants you to ride at her side, so that Dawkins mayn't get at her. Now, Mr. Ingram, I'll bet you half-a-crown I'm at the top of the big Pyramid before you."

Poor Fanny! She obeyed, however; doubtless feeling that it would not do as yet to show too plainly that she preferred Mr. Ingram to her mother. She arrested her donkey, therefore, till Mrs. Damer overtook her; and Mr. Ingram, as he paused for a moment with her while she did so, fell into the hands of Miss Dawkins.

"I cannot think, Fanny, how you get on so quick," said Mrs. Damer. "I'm always last; but then my donkey is such a very nasty one. Look there, now; he's always trying to get me off."

"We shall soon be at the Pyramids now, mamma."

"How on earth I am ever to get back again I cannot think. I am so tired now that I can hardly sit."

"You'll be better, mamma, when you get your luncheon and a glass of wine."

"How on earth we are to eat and drink with those nasty Arab people around us, I can't conceive. They tell me we shall be eaten up by them. But, Fanny, what has Mr. Ingram been saying to you all the day?"

"What has he been saying, mamma? Oh! I don't know;— a hundred things, I dare say. But he has not been talking to me all the time."

"I think he has, Fanny, nearly, since we crossed the river. Oh, dear! oh, dear! this animal does hurt me so! Every time he moves he flings his head about, and that gives me such a bump." And then Fanny commiserated her mother's sufferings, and in her commiseration contrived to elude any further questionings as to Mr. Ingram's conversation.

"Majestic piles, are they not?" said Miss Dawkins, who, having changed her companion, allowed her mind to revert from Mount Sinai to the Pyramids. They were now riding through cultivated ground, with the vast extent of the sands of Libya before them. The two Pyramids were standing on the margin of the sand, with the head of the recumbent sphynx plainly visible between them. But no idea can be formed of the size of this immense figure till it is visited much more closely. The body is covered with sand, and the head and neck alone stand above the surface of the ground. They were still two miles distant, and the sphynx as yet was but an obscure mount between the two vast Pyramids.

"Immense piles!" said Miss Dawkins, repeating her own words.

"Yes, they are large," said Mr. Ingram, who did not choose to indulge in enthusiasm in the presence of Miss Dawkins.

"Enormous! What a grand idea!—eh, Mr. Ingram? The human race does not create such things as those nowadays!"

"No, indeed," he answered; "but perhaps we create better things."

"Better! You do not mean to say, Mr. Ingram, that you are an utilitarian. I do, in truth, hope better things of you than that. Yes! steam mills are better, no doubt, and mechanics' institutes and penny newspapers. But is nothing to be valued but what is useful?" And Miss Dawkins, in the height of her enthusiasm, switched her donkey severely over the shoulder.

"I might, perhaps, have said also that we create more beautiful things," said Mr. Ingram.

"But we cannot create older things."

"No, certainly; we cannot do that."

"Nor can we imbue what we do create with the grand associations which environ those piles with so intense an interest. Think of the mighty dead, Mr. Ingram, and of their great homes when living. Think of the hands which it took to raise those huge blocks—"

"And of the lives which it cost."

"Doubtless. The tyranny and invincible power of the royal architects add to the grandeur of the idea. One would not wish to have back the kings of Egypt."

"Well, no; they would be neither useful nor beautiful."

"Perhaps not; and I do not wish to be picturesque at the expense of my fellow-creatures."

"I doubt, even, whether they would be picturesque."

"You know what I mean, Mr. Ingram. But the associations of such names, and the presence of the stupendous works with which they are connected, fill the soul with awe. Such, at least, is the effect with mine."

"I fear that my tendencies, Miss Dawkins, are more realistic than your own."

"You belong to a young country, Mr. Ingram, and are naturally prone to think of material life. The necessity of living looms large before you."

"Very large, indeed, Miss Dawkins."

"Whereas with us, with some of us at least, the material aspect has given place to one in which poetry and enthusiasm prevail. To such among us the associations of past times are very dear. Cheops, to me, is more than Napoleon Bonaparte."

"That is more than most of your countrymen can say, at any rate, just at present."

"I am a woman," continued Miss Dawkins.

Mr. Ingram took off his hat in acknowledgment both of the announcement and of the fact.

"And to us it is not given—not given as yet—to share in the great deeds of the present. The envy of your sex has driven us from the paths which lead to honour. But the deeds of the past are as much ours as yours."

"Oh, quite as much."

"'Tis to your country that we look for enfranchisement from this thraldom. Yes, Mr. Ingram, the women of America have that strength of mind which has been wanting to those of Europe. In the United States woman will at last learn to exercise her proper mission."

Mr. Ingram expressed a sincere wish that such might be the case; and then wondering at the ingenuity with which Miss Dawkins had travelled round from Cheops and his Pyramid to the rights of women in America, he contrived to fall back, under the pretence of asking after the ailments of Mrs. Damer.

And now at last they were on the sand, in the absolute desert, making their way up to the very foot of the most northern of the two Pyramids. They were by this time surrounded by a crowd of Arab guides, or Arabs professing to be guides, who had already ascertained that Mr. Damer was the chief of the party, and were accordingly driving him almost to madness by the offers of their services, and their assurance that he could not possibly see the outside or the inside of either structure, or even remain alive upon the ground, unless he at once accepted their offers made at their own prices.

"Get away, will you?" said he. "I don't want any of you, and I won't have you! If you take hold of me I'll shoot you!" This was said to one specially energetic Arab, who, in his efforts to secure his prey, had caught hold of Mr. Damer by the leg.

"Yes, yes, I say! Englishmen always take me;—me—me, and then no break him leg. Yes—yes—yes;—I go. Master, say yes. Only one leetle ten shillings!"

"Abdallah!" shouted Mr. Damer, "why don't you take this man away? Why don't you make him understand that if all the Pyramids depended on it, I would not give him sixpence!"

And then Abdallah, thus invoked, came up, and explained to the man in Arabic that he would gain his object more surely if he would behave himself a little more quietly; a hint which the man took for one minute, and for one minute only.

And then poor Mrs. Damer replied to an application for backsheish by the gift of a sixpence. Unfortunate woman! The word backsheish means, I believe, a gift; but it has come in Egypt to signify money, and is eternally dinned into the ears of strangers by Arab suppliants. Mrs. Damer ought to have known better, as, during the last six weeks she had never shown her face out of Shepheard's Hotel without being pestered for backsheish; but she was tired and weak, and foolishly thought to rid herself of the man who was annoying her.

No sooner had the coin dropped from her hand into that of the Arab, than she was surrounded by a cluster of beggars, who loudly made their petitions as though they would, each of them, individually be injured if treated with less liberality than that first comer. They took hold of her donkey, her bridle, her saddle, her legs, and at last her arms and hands, screaming for backsheish in voices that were neither sweet nor mild.

In her dismay she did give away sundry small coins—all, probably, that she had about her; but this only made the matter worse. Money was going, and each man, by sufficient energy, might hope to get some of it. They were very energetic, and so frightened the poor lady that she would certainly have fallen, had she not been kept on her seat by the pressure around her.

"Oh, dear! oh, dear! get away," she cried. "I haven't got any more; indeed I haven't. Go away, I tell you! Mr. Damer! oh, Mr. Damer!" and then, in the excess of her agony, she uttered one loud, long, and continuous shriek.

Up came Mr. Damer; up came Abdallah; up came M. Delabordeau; up came Mr. Ingram, and at last she was rescued. "You shouldn't go away and leave me to the mercy of these nasty people. As to that Abdallah, he is of no use to anybody."

"Why you bodder de good lady, you dem blackguard?" said Abdallah, raising his stick, as though he were going to lay them all low with a blow. "Now you get noting, you tief!"

The Arabs for a moment retired to a little distance, like flies driven from a sugar-bowl; but it was easy to see that, like the flies, they would return at the first vacant moment.

And now they had reached the very foot of the Pyramids and proceeded to dismount from their donkeys. Their intention was first to ascend to the top, then to come down to their banquet, and after that to penetrate into the interior. And all this would seem to be easy of performance. The Pyramid is undoubtedly high, but it is so constructed as to admit of climbing without difficulty. A lady mounting it would undoubtedly need some assistance, but any man possessed of moderate activity would require no aid at all.

But our friends were at once imbued with the tremendous nature of the task before them. A sheikh of the Arabs came forth, who communicated with them through Abdallah. The work could be done, no doubt, he said; but a great many men would be wanted to assist. Each lady must have four Arabs, and each gentlemen three; and then, seeing that the work would be peculiarly severe on this special day, each of these numerous Arabs must be remunerated by some very large number of piastres.

Mr. Damer, who was by no means a close man in his money dealings, opened his eyes with surprise, and mildly expostulated; M. Delabordeau, who was rather a close man in his reckonings, immediately buttoned up his breeches pocket and declared that he should decline to mount the Pyramid at all at that price; and then Mr. Ingram descended to the combat.

The protestations of the men were fearful. They declared, with loud voices, eager actions, and manifold English oaths, that an attempt was being made to rob them. They had a right to demand the sums which they were charging, and it was a shame that English gentlemen should come and take the bread out of their mouths. And so they screeched, gesticulated, and swore, and frightened poor Mrs. Damer almost into fits.

But at last it was settled and away they started, the sheikh declaring that the bargain had been made at so low a rate as to leave him not one piastre for himself. Each man had an Arab on each side of him, and Miss Dawkins and Miss Damer had each, in addition, one behind. Mrs. Damer was so frightened as altogether to have lost all ambition to ascend. She sat below on a fragment of stone, with the three dragomans standing around her as guards; but even with the three dragomans the attacks on her were so frequent, and as she declared afterwards she was so bewildered, that she never had time to remember that she had come there from England to see the Pyramids, and that she was now immediately under them.

The boys, utterly ignoring their guides, scrambled up quicker than the Arabs could follow them. Mr. Damer started off at a pace which soon brought him to the end of his tether, and from that point was dragged up by the sheer strength of his assistants; thereby accomplishing the wishes of the men, who induce their victims to start as rapidly as possible, in order that they may soon find themselves helpless from want of wind. Mr. Ingram endeavoured to attach himself to Fanny, and she would have been nothing loth to have him at her right hand instead of the hideous brown, shrieking, one-eyed Arab who took hold of her. But it was soon found that any such arrangement was impossible. Each guide felt that if he lost his own peculiar hold he would lose his prey, and held on, therefore, with invincible tenacity. Miss Dawkins looked, too, as though she had thought to be attended to by some Christian cavalier, but no Christian cavalier was forthcoming. M. Delabordeau was the wisest, for he took the matter quietly, did as he was bid, and allowed the guides nearly to carry him to the top of the edifice.

"Ha! so this is the top of the Pyramid, is it?" said Mr. Damer, bringing out his words one by one, being terribly out of breath. "Very wonderful, very wonderful, indeed!"

"It is wonderful," said Miss Dawkins, whose breath had not failed her in the least, "very wonderful, indeed! Only think, Mr. Damer, you might travel on for days and days, till days became months, through those interminable sands, and yet you would never come to the end of them. Is it not quite stupendous?"

"Ah, yes, quite,—puff, puff"—said Mr. Damer striving to regain his breath.

Mr. Damer was now at her disposal; weak and worn with toil and travel, out of breath, and with half his manhood gone; if ever she might prevail over him so as to procure from his mouth an assent to that Nile proposition, it would be now. And after all, that Nile proposition was the best one now before her. She did not quite like the idea of starting off across the Great Desert without any lady, and was not sure that she was prepared to be fallen in love with by M. Delabordeau, even if there should ultimately be any readiness on the part of that gentleman to perform the role of lover. With Mr. Ingram the matter was different, nor was she so diffident of her own charms as to think it altogether impossible that she might succeed, in the teeth of that little chit, Fanny Damer. That Mr. Ingram would join the party up the Nile she had very little doubt; and then there would be one place left for her. She would thus, at any rate, become commingled with a most respectable family, who might be of material service to her.

Thus actuated she commenced an earnest attack upon Mr. Damer.

"Stupendous!" she said again, for she was fond of repeating favourite words. "What a wondrous race must have been those Egyptian kings of old!"

"I dare say they were," said Mr. Damer, wiping his brow as he sat upon a large loose stone, a fragment lying on the flat top of the Pyramid, one of those stones with which the complete apex was once made, or was once about to be made.

"A magnificent race! so gigantic in their conceptions! Their ideas altogether overwhelm us poor, insignificant, latter-day mortals. They built these vast Pyramids; but for us, it is task enough to climb to their top."

"Quite enough," ejaculated Mr. Damer.

But Mr. Damer would not always remain weak and out of breath, and it was absolutely necessary for Miss Dawkins to hurry away from Cheops and his tomb, to Thebes and Karnac.

"After seeing this it is impossible for any one with a spark of imagination to leave Egypt without going farther a-field."

Mr. Damer merely wiped his brow and grunted. This Miss Dawkins took as a signal of weakness, and went on with her task perseveringly.

"For myself, I have resolved to go up, at any rate, as far as Asouan and the first cataract. I had thought of acceding to the wishes of a party who are going across the Great Desert by Mount Sinai to Jerusalem; but the kindness of yourself and Mrs. Damer is so great, and the prospect of joining in your boat is so pleasurable, that I have made up my mind to accept your very kind offer."

This, it will be acknowledged, was bold on the part of Miss Dawkins; but what will not audacity effect? To use the slang of modern language, cheek carries everything nowadays. And whatever may have been Miss Dawkins's deficiencies, in this virtue she was not deficient.

"I have made up my mind to accept your very kind offer," she said, shining on Mr. Damer with her blandest smile.

What was a stout, breathless, perspiring, middle-aged gentleman to do under such circumstances? Mr. Damer was a man who, in most matters, had his own way. That his wife should have given such an invitation without consulting him, was, he knew, quite impossible. She would as soon have thought of asking all those Arab guides to accompany them. Nor was it to be thought of that he should allow himself to be kidnapped into such an arrangement by the impudence of any Miss Dawkins. But there was, he felt, a difficulty in answering such a proposition from a young lady with a direct negative, especially while he was so scant of breath. So he wiped his brow again, and looked at her.

"But I can only agree to this on one understanding," continued Miss Dawkins, "and that is, that I am allowed to defray my own full share of the expense of the journey."

Upon hearing this Mr. Damer thought that he saw his way out of the wood. "Wherever I go, Miss Dawkins, I am always the paymaster myself," and this he contrived to say with some sternness, palpitating though he still was; and the sternness which was deficient in his voice he endeavoured to put into his countenance.

But he did not know Miss Dawkins. "Oh, Mr. Damer," she said, and as she spoke her smile became almost blander than it was before; "oh, Mr. Damer, I could not think of suffering you to be so liberal; I could not, indeed. But I shall be quite content that you should pay everything, and let me settle with you in one sum afterwards."

Mr. Damer's breath was now rather more under his own command. "I am afraid, Miss Dawkins," he said, "that Mrs. Damer's weak state of health will not admit of such an arrangement."

"What, about the paying?"

"Not only as to that, but we are a family party, Miss Dawkins; and great as would be the benefit of your society to all of us, in Mrs. Damer's present state of health, I am afraid—in short, you would not find it agreeable.—And therefore—" this he added, seeing that she was still about to persevere—"I fear that we must forego the advantage you offer."

And then, looking into his face, Miss Dawkins did perceive that even her audacity would not prevail.

"Oh, very well," she said, and moving from the stone on which she had been sitting, she walked off, carrying her head very high, to a corner of the Pyramid from which she could look forth alone towards the sands of Libya.

In the mean time another little overture was being made on the top of the same Pyramid,—an overture which was not received quite in the same spirit. While Mr. Damer was recovering his breath for the sake of answering Miss Dawkins, Miss Damer had walked to the further corner of the square platform on which they were placed, and there sat herself down with her face turned towards Cairo. Perhaps it was not singular that Mr. Ingram should have followed her.

This would have been very well if a dozen Arabs had not also followed them. But as this was the case, Mr. Ingram had to play his game under some difficulty. He had no sooner seated himself beside her than they came and stood directly in front of the seat, shutting out the view, and by no means improving the fragrance of the air around them.

"And this, then, Miss Damer, will be our last excursion together," he said, in his tenderest, softest tone.

"De good Englishman will gib de poor Arab one little backsheish," said an Arab, putting out his hand and shaking Mr. Ingram's shoulder.

"Yes, yes, yes; him gib backsheish," said another.

"Him berry good man," said a third, putting up his filthy hand, and touching Mr. Ingram's face.

"And young lady berry good, too; she give backsheish to poor Arab."

"Yes," said a fourth, preparing to take a similar liberty with Miss Damer.

This was too much for Mr. Ingram. He had already used very positive language in his endeavour to assure his tormentors that they would not get a piastre from him. But this only changed their soft persuasions into threats. Upon hearing which, and upon seeing what the man attempted to do in his endeavour to get money from Miss Damer, he raised his stick, and struck first one and then the other as violently as he could upon their heads.

Any ordinary civilised men would have been stunned by such blows, for they fell on the bare foreheads of the Arabs; but the objects of the American's wrath merely skulked away; and the others, convinced by the only arguments which they understood, followed in pursuit of victims who might be less pugnacious.

It is hard for a man to be at once tender and pugnacious—to be sentimental, while he is putting forth his physical strength with all the violence in his power. It is difficult, also, for him to be gentle instantly after having been in a rage. So he changed his tactics at the moment, and came to the point at once in a manner befitting his present state of mind.

"Those vile wretches have put me in such a heat," he said, "that I hardly know what I am saying. But the fact is this, Miss Damer, I cannot leave Cairo without knowing—. You understand what I mean, Miss Damer."

"Indeed I do not, Mr. Ingram; except that I am afraid you mean nonsense."

"Yes, you do; you know that I love you. I am sure you must know it. At any rate you know it now."

"Mr. Ingram, you should not talk in such a way."

"Why should I not? But the truth is, Fanny, I can talk in no other way. I do love you dearly. Can you love me well enough to go and be my wife in a country far away from your own?"

Before she left the top of the Pyramid Fanny Damer had said that she would try.

Mr. Ingram was now a proud and happy man, and seemed to think the steps of the Pyramid too small for his elastic energy. But Fanny feared that her troubles were to come. There was papa—that terrible bugbear on all such occasions. What would papa say? She was sure her papa would not allow her to marry and go so far away from her own family and country. For herself, she liked the Americans—always had liked them; so she said;—would desire nothing better than to live among them. But papa! And Fanny sighed as she felt that all the recognised miseries of a young lady in love were about to fall upon her.

Nevertheless, at her lover's instance, she promised, and declared, in twenty different loving phrases, that nothing on earth should ever make her false to her love or to her lover.

"Fanny, where are you? Why are you not ready to come down?" shouted Mr. Damer, not in the best of tempers. He felt that he had almost been unkind to an unprotected female, and his heart misgave him. And yet it would have misgiven him more had he allowed himself to be entrapped by Miss Dawkins.

"I am quite ready, papa," said Fanny, running up to him—for it may be understood that there is quite room enough for a young lady to run on the top of the Pyramid.

"I am sure I don't know where you have been all the time," said Mr. Damer; "and where are those two boys?"

Fanny pointed to the top of the other Pyramid, and there they were, conspicuous with their red caps.

"And M. Delabordeau?"

"Oh! he has gone down, I think;—no, he is there with Miss Dawkins." And in truth Miss Dawkins was leaning on his arm most affectionately, as she stooped over and looked down upon the ruins below her.

"And where is that fellow, Ingram?" said Mr. Damer, looking about him. "He is always out of the way when he's wanted."

To this Fanny said nothing. Why should she? She was not Mr. Ingram's keeper.

And then they all descended, each again with his proper number of Arabs to hurry and embarrass him; and they found Mr. Damer at the bottom, like a piece of sugar covered with flies. She was heard to declare afterwards that she would not go to the Pyramids again, not if they were to be given to her for herself, as ornaments for her garden.

The picnic lunch among the big stones at the foot of the Pyramid was not a very gay affair. Miss Dawkins talked more than any one else, being determined to show that she bore her defeat gallantly. Her conversation, however, was chiefly addressed to M. Delabordeau, and he seemed to think more of his cold chicken and ham than he did of her wit and attention.

Fanny hardly spoke a word. There was her father before her and she could not eat, much less talk, as she thought of all that she would have to go through. What would he say to the idea of having an American for a son-in-law?

Nor was Mr. Ingram very lively. A young man when he has been just accepted, never is so. His happiness under the present circumstances was, no doubt, intense, but it was of a silent nature.

And then the interior of the building had to be visited. To tell the truth none of the party would have cared to perform this feat had it not been for the honour of the thing. To have come from Paris, New York, or London, to the Pyramids, and then not to have visited the very tomb of Cheops, would have shown on the part of all of them an indifference to subjects of interest which would have been altogether fatal to their character as travellers. And so a party for the interior was made up.

Miss Damer when she saw the aperture through which it was expected that she should descend, at once declared for staying with her mother. Miss Dawkins, however, was enthusiastic for the journey. "Persons with so very little command over their nerves might really as well stay at home," she said to Mr. Ingram, who glowered at her dreadfully for expressing such an opinion about his Fanny.

This entrance into the Pyramids is a terrible task, which should be undertaken by no lady. Those who perform it have to creep down, and then to be dragged up, through infinite dirt, foul smells, and bad air; and when they have done it, they see nothing. But they do earn the gratification of saying that they have been inside a Pyramid.

"Well, I've done that once," said Mr. Damer, coming out, "and I do not think that any one will catch me doing it again. I never was in such a filthy place in my life."

"Oh, Fanny! I am so glad you did not go; I am sure it is not fit for ladies," said poor Mrs. Damer, forgetful of her friend Miss Dawkins.

"I should have been ashamed of myself," said Miss Dawkins, bristling up, and throwing back her head as she stood, "if I had allowed any consideration to have prevented my visiting such a spot. If it be not improper for men to go there, how can it be improper for women?"

"I did not say improper, my dear," said Mrs. Damer, apologetically.

"And as for the fatigue, what can a woman be worth who is afraid to encounter as much as I have now gone through for the sake of visiting the last resting-place of such a king as Cheops?" And Miss Dawkins, as she pronounced the last words, looked round her with disdain upon poor Fanny Damer.

"But I meant the dirt," said Mrs. Damer.

"Dirt!" ejaculated Miss Dawkins, and then walked away. Why should she now submit her high tone of feeling to the Damers, or why care longer for their good opinion?

Therefore she scattered contempt around her as she ejaculated the last word, "dirt."

And then the return home! "I know I shall never get there," said Mrs. Damer, looking piteously up into her husband's face.

"Nonsense, my dear; nonsense; you must get there." Mrs. Damer groaned, and acknowledged in her heart that she must,—either dead or alive.

"And, Jefferson," said Fanny, whispering—for there had been a moment since their descent in which she had been instructed to call him by his Christian name— "never mind talking to me going home. I will ride by mamma. Do you go with papa and put him in good humour; and it he says anything about the lords and the bishops, don't you contradict him, you know."

What will not a man do for love? Mr. Ingram promised.

And in this way they started; the two boys led the van; then came Mr. Damer and Mr. Ingram, unusually and unpatriotically acquiescent as to England's aristocratic propensities; then Miss Dawkins riding, alas! alone; after her, M. Delabordeau, also alone,—the ungallant Frenchman! And the rear was brought up by Mrs. Damer and her daughter, flanked on each side by a dragoman, with a third dragoman behind them.

And in this order they went back to Cairo, riding their donkeys, and crossing the ferry solemnly, and, for the most part, silently. Mr. Ingram did talk, as he had an important object in view,—that of putting Mr. Damer into a good humour.

In this he succeeded so well that by the time they had remounted, after crossing the Nile, Mr. Damer opened his heart to his companion on the subject that was troubling him, and told him all about Miss Dawkins.

"I don't see why we should have a companion that we don't like for eight or ten weeks, merely because it seems rude to refuse a lady."

"Indeed, I agree with you," said Mr. Ingram; "I should call it weak—minded to give way in such a case."

"My daughter does not like her at all," continued Mr. Damer.

"Nor would she be a nice companion for Miss Damer; not according to my way of thinking," said Mr. Ingram.

"And as to my having asked her, or Mrs. Damer having asked her! Why, God bless my soul, it is pure invention on the woman's part!"

"Ha! ha! ha!" laughed Mr. Ingram; "I must say she plays her game well; but then she is an old soldier, and has the benefit of experience." What would Miss Dawkins have said had she known that Mr. Ingram called her an old soldier?

"I don't like the kind of thing at all," said Mr. Damer, who was very serious upon the subject. "You see the position in which I am placed. I am forced to be very rude, or—"

"I don't call it rude at all."

"Disobliging, then; or else I must have all my comfort invaded and pleasure destroyed by, by, by—" And Mr. Damer paused, being at a loss for an appropriate name for Miss Dawkins.

"By an unprotected female," suggested Mr. Ingram.

"Yes, just so. I am as fond of pleasant company as anybody; but then I like to choose it myself."

"So do I," said Mr. Ingram, thinking of his own choice.

"Now, Ingram, if you would join us, we should be delighted."

"Upon my word, sir, the offer is too flattering," said Ingram, hesitatingly; for he felt that he could not undertake such a journey until Mr. Damer knew on what terms he stood with Fanny.

"You are a terrible democrat," said Mr. Damer, laughing; "but then, on that matter, you know, we could agree to differ."

"Exactly so," said Mr. Ingram, who had not collected his thoughts or made up his mind as to what he had better say and do, on the spur of the moment.

"Well, what do you say to it?" said Mr. Damer, encouragingly. But Ingram paused before he answered.

"For Heaven's sake, my dear fellow, don't have the slightest hesitation in refusing, if you don't like the plan."

"The fact is, Mr. Damer, I should like it too well."

"Like it too well?"

"Yes, sir, and I may as well tell you now as later. I had intended this evening to have asked for your permission to address your daughter."

"God bless my soul!" said Mr. Damer, looking as though a totally new idea had now been opened to him.

"And under these circumstances, I will now wait and see whether or no you will renew your offer."

"God bless my soul!" said Mr. Damer, again. It often does strike an old gentleman as very odd that any man should fall in love with his daughter, whom he has not ceased to look upon as a child. The case is generally quite different with mothers. They seem to think that every young man must fall in love with their girls.

"And have you said anything to Fanny about this?" asked Mr. Damer.

"Yes, sir, I have her permission to speak to you."

"God bless my soul!" said Mr. Damer; and by this time they had arrived at Shepheard's Hotel.

"Oh, mamma," said Fanny, as soon as she found herself alone with her mother that evening, "I have something that I must tell you."

"Oh, Fanny, don't tell me anything to-night, for I am a great deal too tired to listen."

"But oh, mamma, pray;—you must listen to this; indeed you must." And Fanny knelt down at her mother's knee, and looked beseechingly up into her face.

"What is it, Fanny? You know that all my bones are sore, and I am so tired that I am almost dead."

"Mamma, Mr. Ingram has—"

"Has what, my dear? has he done anything wrong?"

"No, mamma: but he has;—he has proposed to me." And Fanny, bursting into tears, hid her face in her mother's lap.

And thus the story was told on both sides of the house. On the next day, as a matter of course, all the difficulties and dangers of such a marriage as that which was now projected were insisted on by both father and mother.

It was improper; it would cause a severing of the family not to be thought of; it would be an alliance of a dangerous nature, and not at all calculated to insure happiness; and, in short, it was impossible. On that day, therefore, they all went to bed very unhappy. But on the next day, as was also a matter of course, seeing that there were no pecuniary difficulties, the mother and father were talked over, and Mr. Ingram was accepted as a son-in-law. It need hardly be said that the offer of a place in Mr. Damer's boat was again made, and that on this occasion it was accepted without hesitation.

There was an American Protestant clergyman resident in Cairo, with whom, among other persons, Miss Dawkins had become acquainted. Upon this gentleman or upon his wife Miss Dawkins called a few days after the journey to the Pyramid, and finding him in his study, thus performed her duty to her neighbour,—

"You know your countryman Mr. Ingram, I think?" said she.

"Oh, yes; very intimately."

"If you have any regard for him, Mr. Burton," such was the gentleman's name, "I think you should put him on his guard."

"On his guard against what?" said Mr. Burton with a serious air, for there was something serious in the threat of impending misfortune as conveyed by Miss Dawkins.

"Why," said she, "those Damers, I fear, are dangerous people."

"Do you mean that they will borrow money of him?"

"Oh, no; not that, exactly; but they are clearly setting their cap at him."

"Setting their cap at him?"

"Yes; there is a daughter, you know; a little chit of a thing; and I fear Mr. Ingram may be caught before he knows where he is. It would be such a pity, you know. He is going up the river with them, I hear. That, in his place, is very foolish. They asked me, but I positively refused."

Mr. Burton remarked that "In such a matter as that Mr. Ingram would be perfectly able to take care of himself."

"Well, perhaps so; but seeing what was going on, I thought it my duty to tell you." And so Miss Dawkins took her leave.

Mr. Ingram did go up the Nile with the Damers, as did an old friend of the Damers who arrived from England. And a very pleasant trip they had of it. And, as far as the present historian knows, the two lovers were shortly afterwards married in England.

Poor Miss Dawkins was left in Cairo for some time on her beam ends. But she was one of those who are not easily vanquished. After an interval of ten days she made acquaintance with an Irish family—having utterly failed in moving the hard heart of M. Delabordeau—and with these she proceeded to Constantinople. They consisted of two brothers and a sister, and were, therefore, very convenient for matrimonial purposes. But nevertheless, when I last heard of Miss Dawkins, she was still an unprotected female.

LaVergne, TN USA
26 April 2010
180551LV00001B/66/P